Christm

Yes, it is—

All our stories th.. ....olve
children at Christmas time, as the adults in their
lives try their very best to make the festive season
as happy as possible for the little, and not so
little, ones concerned, while finding their own
special person to love. And sometimes the kids
work a little magic of their own, for the best
present of all is to become a family.

Our four authors bring you their family traditions
from around the world. We visit America with
Jessica Matthews, Australia with Meredith
Webber, South Africa with Elisabeth Scott and
England with Caroline Anderson. The different
types of weather in these countries make no
difference to the warmth of the Season's
Greeting we send to you.

Dear Reader

My earliest memory of Christmas is a white one. I remember snowball fights with my sister, and having uncles and aunts and cousins for Christmas Day, and decorating the tree on Christmas Eve and waking up at some ungodly hour to see what was in my stocking. Satsuma in the toe, apple in the heel, orange at the top and nuts and chocolates and several little presents in between—it never changed. The first year I was considered too old to have a stocking was awful. It just didn't seem like Christmas, despite the 'real' presents under the tree. I wasn't ready to grow up!

I've had to now, of course, because I'm chief cook and bottle-washer. We always have relatives, and eat at one—or aim to! We always watch the Queen and lie in front of the fire with the dog. It never changes. I hope it never will.

Wherever you are, and whatever your traditions, I hope you enjoy the book and have a really terrific day. Merry Christmas!

Caroline Anderson

A VERY SPECIAL NEED

BY
CAROLINE ANDERSON

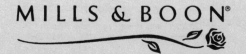

MILLS & BOON®

For all at Gilmour Piper & Associates
who have been so patient; for Judith Westmore and the
R.D.A.
and for Pipkin

*First published in Great Britain 1997
Harlequin Mills & Boon Limited,
Eton House, 18-24 Paradise Road, Richmond, Surrey TW9 1SR*

© Caroline Anderson 1997

ISBN 0 263 80513 1

*Set in Times 10 on 11 pt. by
Rowland Phototypesetting Limited
Bury St Edmunds, Suffolk*

03-9712-49876-D

*Printed and bound in Great Britain
by Mackays of Chatham PLC, Chatham*

CHAPTER ONE

'HAPPY birthday.'

'Thanks.'

'Thirty today and still looking as good as ever.'

Judith gave her reflection a jaundiced sneer. 'You're biased,' she told it. 'And a lousy liar.'

The reflection sneered back—the little snub nose wrinkling, the eyes unflinching—taking inventory with no holds barred. They scanned the skin, pale under the superficial light tan of summer, and the eyes smudged with shadows of worry and fatigue—the laughter lines unused in recent weeks. Hmm, she thought. The bone structure was all right, but the top dressing lacked a certain sparkle, and the hair today was definitely mouse brown.

The eyes scanned down her body over the soft curves that despite the scrimped diet failed to disappear, assessing the charity shop clothes—the clever buys that managed to look almost reasonable if not at the cutting edge of fashion—then back up, meeting themselves with relentless honesty.

'OK,' the reflection conceeded. 'So you're looking thirty today. And tired. And jaded, and dissatisfied with your lot. And you've got a white hair—see it there, sticking out?'

She turned away from the unblinking grey lasers. She didn't need that much honesty, even from herself—and especially not today.

Thirty, she thought, and what had she got to show for it? She looked round the living room of the small flat, at the furniture that, like her, looked tired and jaded and dissatisfied. A rented home, second-hand furniture, Oxfam clothes, temporary work in the term time to keep them ticking over—she had nothing to show for her thirty years at all.

There was a shuffling, bumping noise in the hall.

No. Not nothing, she amended. She had Edward—and she hadn't even managed to do that right.

She turned a bright smile to the door as it swung open. 'All ready?'

He nodded, slowly and deliberately, and his mouth twisted into a parody of a smile. His eyes went from her to the mirror just beside her. 'Looking for the wrinkles?' he teased in his halting, reluctant speech.

'Cheeky monkey,' she said with a grin, and went over and hugged him. 'All ready for school?'

'I suppose so.'

She eyed him worriedly. 'Want to talk about it?'

He shrugged, a slow, deliberate shrug that matched his other movements. 'New kids—nothing I can't handle.'

New kids looking at him, wondering what was wrong with him, calling him 'Spaz' and laughing at his hesitant speech and awkward gait. The first day of the new school year was always the same. A wave of maternal protectiveness almost swamped her, but she crushed it back down ruthlessly. He didn't need her pity.

'You'll be fine,' she assured him briskly. 'They'll soon get used to you and they won't think anything of it in a week or so—less if they join the chess club.'

He grinned, his courage as always bringing tears very close to the surface. She turned away and gathered up her bag and a light jacket against the chilly September wind, and blinked hard.

'Let's go, then,' she said, turning back with her smile firmly in place again. 'And tonight we'll have a treat and go out for a pizza.'

'Can we afford it?' he asked with a shrewd wisdom well ahead of his thirteen years.

She punched his arm gently. 'Hey, you let me worry about that. It's my birthday—we ought to celebrate.'

'Yeah.' His smile was sad, and he shifted his school bag on his shoulder and turned, picking up his sticks from by the door. 'Let's hit the road, then.'

They walked down the path and turned left, coming out within a minute or so onto the road along which the bus ran. There was a crowd of youngsters gathered at the stop, and she could feel the tension pouring off him as he braced himself and walked towards them.

'See you, Mum,' he mumbled, and she made herself hang back and watch from a distance as he joined the group.

A black boy separated from the crowd, tall and gangling in baggy jeans, his head completely shaved. 'Yo, Woody, how you doin', man?' he yelled and gave her son a high five, then flung an arm around his shoulders and dragged him into the crowd.

She grinned to herself and turned away. He'd be all right now. Al would take care of him. Al's baby sister had cerebral palsy, too—the double disadvantage of being black *and* disabled. Al understood Woody—and Al was a good kid with a heart of gold, even if his hairstyle made Judith flinch. Yes, he'd take care of her son.

And who would take care of her? She stifled a sigh, tugged her jacket closer against the wind and walked briskly towards town and the job centre. Term time meant finding a job to hold body and soul together—and she'd have to find one or there was no way she dared to take Woody out tonight for a pizza, or it might be the last meal they ate for a long, long while.

'So, how was it?'

He shrugged. 'OK. I've got Mr Greenhill for Maths.'

Her eyebrows shot up and pride surged in her chest. 'Really? Well done.'

She watched as he pulled off another slice of pizza and wrapped his tongue round the trails of stretchy cheese, hooking it into his mouth with conscious deliberation.

'It's no big deal. I can do the work easily.'

She smiled. 'I know.'

He pushed the pizza towards her. 'Here. You've only had one bit.'

'I'm not hungry,' she lied. 'You eat it.'

He put the slice down and met her grey eyes with his blue ones. 'Did you get a job?'

She swallowed the fear that seemed to grow ever larger in her chest. 'Uh—not today. They've got another one or two they're looking into for me,' she lied, and wondered if her thirties were going to be remembered for the number and range of lies she was to tell her son.

'Something will turn up,' she promised him, and to take the worry out of his eyes she picked up the slice of pizza she'd meant to save for her lunch tomorrow and ate it. As it was they had bought one from the supermarket to save money rather than go to the Pizza Hut, and she'd only done that because she'd promised him pizza and the fresh ones from the supermarket were nearly as nice and not quite as expensive.

Tomorrow would be sausages or mince or fish fingers as usual.

Please, God, she thought, let me find a job.

'How about a game of chess?' she suggested brightly.

Woody eyed her sceptically. 'Does that mean I have to let you win because it's your birthday?'

'Cheeky monkey. I might beat you anyway.'

He grinned, lopsided and teasing. 'Yeah. After all, there's always room in the world for another miracle.'

She chuckled, cleared away the pizza plates and put the chess board on the table. 'Right, you, do your worst,' she challenged, and wondered, if there was a spare miracle lying around, whether it could please be dedicated to her finding a job and not thrashing her cocky son at chess. . .

Nothing was ever easy. There was no job, neither the next day nor the one afterwards, and on the Thursday evening Woody was late back from the bus. She was walking down the path to investigate when he came into view, walking even more awkwardly and his face twisted with pain.

'Woody? Whatever's wrong?' she asked, running the last few steps towards him.

'I fell,' he said tersely. He looked withdrawn and mutinous, and she could tell he was suffering.

'OK. Let's get you in and inspect the damage. I want to hear all about it.'

'I'm fine, I just fell,' he repeated, limping painfully up the little step to their front door.

Judith doubted that he 'just' fell. Oh, he did sometimes genuinely fall, of course. She knew that. She also knew that look on his face, that stubborn, determined look which overtook him when someone had cut him to the bone—just as she knew that there was more to this than a simple fall, but she could do nothing.

To interfere and fuss would simply make it worse.

'Cup of tea?' she offered, allowing him to deal with it in his way.

'Mmm, please.' He sat at the kitchen table, a muffled groan escaping from his tightly closed mouth, and she shut her eyes and counted to ten.

She put the mug down in front of him. 'Here. Drink this while I run you a hot bath,' she said softly, and went out before she gave in to the urge to cry her eyes out.

He didn't deserve this—whatever 'this' was. Life was tough enough without some bully going for him. She wondered if he would ever tell her what had really happened.

He wouldn't let her help him with the bath. That didn't surprise her. He'd been independent in that department for some years now, struggling to cope alone while she metaphorically bit her nails on the other side of the door.

This time, though, he was ages and she could hear the groans from the kitchen.

There was a time for his pride, she decided, and a time when she just had to be a mother.

She waited until he had gone into his bedroom, then knocked on the door.

'What?' he growled.

'Edward, I want to come in.'

The door opened to reveal her son, clad only in a pair of briefs and some colourful bruises. 'Why do you always call me Edward when you want to pull rank?' he said mildly, and turned away.

She swallowed a retort and studied his body. Thin, a little twisted, never moving smoothly, it was even more stiff and jerky than usual tonight. She ran her practised eye over him, looking for strains and stresses, and her eyes settled on his spine.

'Have you put your back out, falling?'

He nodded. 'I'll live.'

'I don't doubt it. Where did you fall?' She tried to keep the edge of irony out of her voice but failed.

'On the stairs,' he told her defiantly. 'I tripped over my foot.'

Plausible but not the truth. Her son could never lie to her, she knew him far too well. Sure, he'd tripped over a foot, but whose? 'I'll bring you some ibuprofen tablets.'

'I'll come. I've got homework to do,' he told her, and followed her a few painful minutes later, dressed in a baggy tracksuit which hung on his gaunt frame. Heavens, he was getting so tall now. . .

'How about your physio?' she suggested, wondering if that would give her an opportunity to find out how hurt he really was.

'I don't think so. Not tonight. Perhaps tomorrow.'

It must be bad, she thought. Painful as his physio was, he never shirked the chore they had shared each evening for so many years.

She went in to his room to tuck him up and turn off his light at ten. He was asleep, his lashes black against the pale, drawn cheeks. He looked so fragile. She brushed the thick dark hair away from his brow and dropped a kiss on his cheek, surprised yet again at the fine dark fuzz that covered his jaw. He would need to start shaving soon, she realised with a shock.

He was growing up so fast. Up and out and away from her, his battle for independence every bit as fierce as any other teenager's, only the other kids didn't have to deal with disability as well.

'I love you,' she whispered soundlessly. 'Please don't be hurt.'

In the morning he could hardly walk. Knowing his courage and knowing from her own experience that bad backs were best treated by specialists, she sent him back to bed and left the flat.

In the next street, just a few hundred yards away, there was an osteopath. As well as being so convenient for her home, he had also established an excellent reputation. She had heard his name at several clinics and support group meetings, and she understood he treated lots of children with cerebral palsy and other disabilities. Not that she could afford any treatment, more's the pity. No, but she would go and ask his advice. Hopefully it would be free.

It was a strange area, she thought as she set off. Their flat was a maisonette, the lower half of a conventional-looking two storey house in a little street with several similar ones, drab and ordinary but functional. Aesthetic appeal seemed to have passed it by, and yet round the corner the next street was altogether grander, the houses imposing Victorian double fronted status symbols, very des-res and so far out of her reach that she hardly even dared to imagine what they were like inside.

At the entrance to one of them she hesitated, looking up at the impressive red-brick façade, at the large bay windows and ornate stone lintels and the immaculate garden with shrubs and perennials creeping onto the tar-macked drive in carefully orchestrated profusion.

It was gorgeous—and intimidating. It was also the home and workplace of the man she wanted to talk to. Mentally girding her loins, she walked up the driveway, past the cars parked at the front, and found the outer door propped open. Beyond the glass door into the hall she saw a reception desk ahead of her, a beautiful walnut desk with the glorious patina of age. It was probably worth more than her entire flat contents.

Her heart sank. This man was weathly and successful. Why should he help her? She was about to turn tail and run when the receptionist, a woman of about Judith's own age, looked up and smiled through the glass, and beckoned her in.

She went. It would have been impossibly rude not to have done so, and she dredged up an answering smile.

'Good morning,' the receptionist said as she approached. 'Can I help you?'

Where to start? How about the obvious? she thought. 'My name's Judith Wright. I wonder if it would be poss-ible for me to have a word with Mr Barber about my son.'

'Is he a new patient?' the woman asked, turning to a card index on the desk. Judith noticed that she was very pregnant. His wife?

'No. Well, that is, he isn't a patient—not yet. That

was what I wanted to discuss,' she lied boldly.

The woman smiled. 'I see. If you'd like to take a seat, Mrs Wright, I'll have a word with him in a few minutes in between patients.'

She didn't bother to correct the mistake. She was so used to being called Mrs Wright that she ignored it now. Returning the smile, Judith went through the door indicated and found herself in a waiting room overlooking the front. It was light, airy and welcoming—and most of the chairs were upright, wooden armchairs, ideal for people with bad backs, she thought with a slight smile. She armed herself with a magazine and sat in one of the chairs. There were two other people in there, a man and a woman sitting on opposite sides of the room, their noses buried in magazines.

She looked round the elegant, high-ceilinged room with the ornate plaster cornice and beautiful marble fireplace with a lovely iron and tiled centre. It was a wonderful room, she thought. The decor was subdued but effective, soft smoky green colour-washing below the dado rail and a very traditional stripe above, with the green echoed on the ceiling and the plasterwork picked out in off-white. The muted brick tones of the carpet warmed the scheme and gave it colour, reflected in the curtain fabric and the tiles of the fireplace. Very clever. Very effective. Very restful. She wondered who had chosen the scheme. His wife? The receptionist?

No. Probably a fancy interior designer who had been paid a fortune. She glanced at her watch and wondered how long she would have to wait. Ten minutes? Fifteen? Perhaps until both of these patients had been treated—if he would even see her then—

'Mrs Wright?'

She looked up—straight into a pair of the most startlingly blue eyes she had ever seen—and felt a jolt of something that rocked her to the core.

Lightning? If she hadn't felt so shaken by it, she might have laughed. She didn't laugh, though. She couldn't. She stood up, pulled to her feet by the power of those astonishing eyes, and crossed the room, dropping the magazine absently on the table as she passed it.

'Hugh Barber,' he said by way of introduction, and held out his hand. She took it, her own engulfed by the powerful fingers in a firm and yet gentle handshake. Their palms met briefly, and she dropped his hand at once, shocked by the searing heat. No, not heat. Warmth, and something else—something big and strong and comforting that made her want to bury her head against that solid chest just in front of her eyes and give in to all the anguish and worry and torment of the past fourteen years.

She didn't, though. By a miracle she managed to avoid hurling herself into his unsuspecting arms and went through the door he indicated. The room was the mirror image of the one she had just been in, the colours a similar soft, muted green and cream, designed for relaxing in.

Judith didn't feel relaxed. She was about to do something she hated doing, and she could feel the tension coiled in her like a watchspring. He waved her to a chair beside the desk, perched on the treatment couch with one leg dangling and smiled encouragingly at her.

'I gather you wanted to talk to me about your son,' he said, and his voice swirled through her like dark chocolate.

She looked down at her hands to avoid those searching, stunning eyes. 'Yes. He's had a fall—he says he tripped. He's got mild cerebral palsy—he is a little clumsy at times, but I think this was deliberate. Whatever, his back's injured in some way—jarred. I wondered if you could tell me what I should do to help him.'

'Of course. I'll have to see him, obviously. I have a children's clinic on the other side of town on Tuesdays. Is that any good to you?'

She grimaced slightly. 'Transport's difiicult,' she told him, hoping that would be enough. It wasn't.

'I'll see him here, then, if it's easier. Have a word with my receptionist and she'll make you an appointment. I take it you are able to get here?'

'We only live round the corner, but just at the moment I don't know that he could walk that far. I'll have to see,' she flannelled. 'If you could just give me some advice initially. . .'

'I really should see him to be on the safe side. Have you taken him to the hospital for an X-ray?'

'Um—no. I'm sure he's just jarred it. There's nothing broken.'

'Then if you could manage to get him in to me—perhaps a taxi?'

Damn. He wasn't going to just give her advice, that was clear. She swallowed. A taxi was totally out of the question. Al's mother, Belle, might be able to give them a lift if she wasn't working, but she was a community midwife and worked strange hours—as well as juggling Al and Flora as a single parent.

No. She couldn't ask Belle. 'We'll manage. We've got a wheelchair we can use.' Judith drew in a steadying breath, lifted her head and met the man's searching eyes. He seemed to be waiting, as if he knew there was something to follow—something difficult and awkward and embarrassing. She hated what she was going to have to do, but she'd do it for Woody.

'I haven't got any money,' she told him with quiet dignity. 'I'm hoping to get a job soon for the term. I wondered. . .' she swallowed '. . .if you would be able to bill me for the treatment and let me pay you back as I earn the money.'

There. It was said. She held his eyes, resisting the urge to run away, and brazened it out.

*　　*　　*

Hugh looked deep into the challenging eyes of this gutsy little woman daring him to turn her down, and wondered at the hurdles she'd had to overcome and the struggles she'd had to face.

There was such determination in the jut of her chin and the tilt of her head, such uncertainty deep in those lovely, soft grey eyes. What had she had to cope with? She hadn't said how old her son was, but he guessed around ten, probably. She looked as if she was in her early thirties—maybe not that old if life had been cruel.

He was sure it had. Life was. His own had been cruel, leaving the indelible marks of grief etched on his face. It didn't hurt so much now, but it had and the scars showed.

Mrs Wright had scars, too—worry and strain engraved on such soft, fine skin that it seemed a travesty. His fingers ached to soothe away the worry.

That wasn't all that ached. For the first time in what must be years, he felt attracted to a woman, not only physically but somewhere deeper in the hidden recesses of his subconscious. When he'd touched her he'd felt the most unbelievable warmth flow through his hand. He'd never felt anything like it before. It was more than simple sexual chemistry. It felt almost like—destiny?

Lord, he was going nuts. Anyway, inevitably she was married to the probably undeserving Mr Wright. Hugh wondered if the lucky dog realised just how lucky he was. If not, he wondered if there was some other fortunate ingrate keeping this lovely woman warm at night.

He felt a sharp, shocking twist of something which could only be jealousy. Good grief! What on earth was the matter with him?

Anyway, he'd probably imagined his reaction and, even if not, it was almost certainly not reciprocated.

He curled his fingers over his still-tingling palm and got back to the reason for her visit.

'How old is your son, Mrs Wright?'

'Thirteen—and it's Miss. I'm a single parent.'

He ruthlessly suppressed the urge to whoop with delight. 'And has he had any back trouble before?'

'Aches and pains—nothing the physio and I couldn't keep under control.'

'And what makes you think he needs to see an osteopath and not a physiotherapist this time?' Hugh asked, curious about her motives.

'Experience. I know him, and I know the limitations of physio. I also know about bad backs to an extent. There are times when nothing else works.'

'And you think this is one of those times?' Hugh pressed.

'Yes, I do.'

Even her voice was wonderful. Soft, well modulated, almost a caress. He forced himself to stop fantasising and engaging her in needless conversation, and got to the point.

'It may take several treatments.'

She swallowed. 'I know.'

He nodded. 'OK,' he murmured. 'I'm sure we can stagger the payments if that will help you,' he told her, and was rewarded by the bright glimmer of tears in her eyes before she dropped her head forwards.

'Thank you,' she whispered.

He stood up, angry with himself for dragging out her misery and making her justify herself just so he could hear her voice. 'Have a word with my receptionist—I can probably fit him in at lunchtime today so he doesn't have to wait over the weekend. I'm sorry, I'm going to have to press on, I've got a patient waiting. I'll see you both later.'

He watched her walk over to Christine, closed his eyes briefly to clear his mind of the sensual image burnt on

his retinas and stuck his head round the waiting-room
door. 'Mrs Parker, would you come in, please?'

Woody found even the wheelchair difficult. Sitting was
nearly as bad as walking, and by the time they arrived at
the lovely red-brick house he was tight-lipped with pain.

He still managed a smile for her, though, as she
wheeled him in. Lord, he was a gutsy kid. Judith looked
away from him, her eyes bright with tears, and found
herself face to face with the man whose image she had
been unable to get out of her mind since this morning.

'Hi,' he said cheerfully, then hunkered down beside
Woody. 'You must be Edward. Pleased to meet you. I
gather you've hurt your back?'

Woody mumbled a response, and Judith watched as
they shook hands, then Mr Barber looked up at her. 'I
wonder if you'd mind filling in a card with all Edward's
details while we go and have a chat and I have a quick
look to see what he's done to himself?'

He gave her a card, a pen and a wink, and disappeared
into his consulting room, pushing her son ahead of him
in the wheelchair. She chewed her lip. Should she be in
there with him?

She'd been clearly dismissed. Oh, well, perhaps he'd
have some joy getting the truth out of him without her
hovering about being a fussy mother.

She sat down with the card and obediently filled in all
the information.

'So, Edward, I gather you fell down some stairs, is that
right, and now your back hurts?'

The boy nodded slowly. He certainly had quite a bit
of spasticity in his muscles, Hugh noted. His handshake
had been slow and deliberate but strong, and Hugh knew
the hardest part of the treatment would be getting the

muscles to relax enough to allow him to work on the spine.

Inevitably after thirteen years there would be some deformity and contracture problems. Just how bad and how insurmountable, he would have to establish. 'I wonder if you could stand up and let me take a look at you?' he murmured.

Woody struggled out of the chair, wincing as his back twinged, and Hugh forced himself to stand back and observe. One shoulder was a little higher than the other, indicating a slight scoliosis—a sideways curve to his spine which would be more obvious, of course, without clothes—but basically his posture was better than Hugh had expected.

'OK. If you could just slip off your clothes down to your pants I'll go and see how your mother's getting on. Do you want her to join us?'

The boy shrugged, a slow, deliberate shrug, his face expressionless.

'I think we can probably manage without her, don't you? I'll give her a cup of tea and we can get started.'

He left the lad undressing and went to find Judith. She was sitting in the waiting room with her head bent forwards, resting on a book on her knee while she filled in the record card. Her bottom lip was caught between small, even white teeth in an endearing little gesture that tugged at something inside him. The sun caught her hair, gleaming off the red-gold lights in it, and he had to fight against the urge to pull the band off the back and tunnel his fingers through it, fanning it out over her shoulders and spreading it across the crisp white pillow—

He yanked himself up short, shocked by the unruly direction of his thoughts, and cleared his throat. She looked up, straight into his eyes, and he had the sudden ghastly feeling that she could read his sordid mind. 'Ah—how are you doing?' he asked, conscious of the slow crawl of heat up the back of his neck.

'All done,' she replied, her voice soft and husky and unbelievably sexy. 'I was just checking it.'

'Good.' He cleared his throat again and took the card from her outstretched hand, carefully avoiding touching her. 'Look, I think your son might appreciate it if I treat him without you there?' He phrased it almost as a question, to give her the chance to discuss it, but to his relief she nodded.

'I rather thought you wanted to. Perhaps you'll be able to find out what really happened.'

'That's what I was thinking,' he told her honestly. 'Obviously he doesn't want you to know the truth because he doesn't want you hurt by it, and he knows you would be.'

Her smile nearly blew a fuse in his mind. 'I'm so glad you understand,' she said fervently. 'They're so convoluted, kids.'

He grinned at her. 'I make an art form of understanding teenage boys—I've got one of my own. Look, I tell you what, you sit here and have a cup of tea while I get to grips with Edward. OK?'

She looked astonished, her eyes wide and soft and grateful. 'Um—fine. Thank you.'

'How do you take your tea?'

'White, no sugar.'

'Right.' He escaped, almost running down the hall to the kitchen. Christine was sitting on the sofa with her feet up, resting her hands on the smooth swell of her pregnancy.

'Hi. Any tea in the pot for Miss Wright?'

'Should be. Hugh, my back's giving me hell—I don't suppose you could have a go at it, could you? It's been dodgy all day again.'

He looked across at her. She seemed pinched, a bit tired. Hell. He really must find another receptionist so she could start her maternity leave—

'I'll just get this kid out of the way and I'll have a look at you then, I promise. You stay here and take it easy for a few minutes—get some shut-eye. Oh, and while I think about it, Edward Wright's bill is going to be staggered and I'm going to tell her I charge half-price for children under sixteen.'

Christine managed a wan smile. 'Softy,' she murmured.

He grinned. 'That's me. Just a sucker for a sob-story. Rest now. I won't be long.'

She nodded, and he took the tea back to the waiting room and handed it to Edward's mother. 'Here—one cup of tea, white, no sugar.'

'Thanks.' She flashed that dazzling smile at him again, and he had to swallow hard and dredge in a great lungful of air before he could make his legs work again. How his system could have gone from years of near-coma to absolute screaming wakefulness in such a short time, he didn't know, but it certainly had.

He shook his head to clear it, went back into his consulting room and shut the door. There, propped against the edge of the couch in some pain, was the reason this beautiful woman had come into his life—the only reason, he reminded himself—and he would do well to remember it.

'Right, Edward, let's see what we can do for you,' he said briskly, and banished his intrusive libido from his thoughts.

CHAPTER TWO

'RIGHT, Edward, if you could stand up and turn round
so I can see your back, perhaps we'll be able to sort this
pain out a bit for you. Can you tell me where it hurts?'

The boy put a finger on his back, just below his waist
and slightly to one side, over the lumbosacral joint which
linked his flexible spine to the less flexible ring of his
pelvis. It was a common spot for difficulties, being the
junction between the two areas and so subject to more
stresses than the other joints.

Hugh watched as Edward bent slowly forwards, tipped
sideways, rotated, straightened up and tipped back, gener-
ally showing a grossly restricted range of movement in
that whole area. It wasn't all due to the current injury—
that much Hugh could see at a glance—but certainly the
injury was compromising the movement Edward did
have, and making the situation much worse.

'Right, if you could lie on the couch for me on your
right side facing me,' he said, making it perfectly obvious
which way he wanted the boy to lie by taking up his
position beside the couch, and waited to see if he was
able to follow instructions.

He could tell by the brightness of his eyes and the few
things he had said that he was certainly intelligent. How
much his brain had been damaged in the trauma which
had caused his cerebral palsy Hugh didn't know, but he
wanted to find out for himself and not from the boy's
mother. He wanted no preconceptions.

Edward lay down exactly as asked, and when Hugh
bent his knees up, propped them against his hip and
rocked the boy gently, curling and uncurling his spine

22

with slow, careful movements, he could feel the pull of the taut, spastic muscles fighting him all the way. 'I just want to get this area moving a little,' he explained. 'See if I can get some freedom back into this joint.' He supported the spine with the flat of his hand, rocked away gently for a while and gradually the muscles began to give a little and he was able to get more movement through the joint.

'It's very tight, isn't it?' he said to Edward. 'Is it often?'

'It always is,' the boy replied. 'I have a lot of spasticity in my psoas muscles as well.'

No flies on this kid, Hugh thought with interest as he worked on the tight muscles. What a damn shame he'd been damaged at birth. He made a mental note to ask Judith—no, Miss Wright—the circumstances. 'Who does your physio?' he asked.

'Mum—and the physio comes to school once a week to see how things are going. I have a special session with her when the others have got games.'

'Do you do any games?

'I work out in the gym a little with some special exercises when the others are there, but I can't play football, of course. I go riding on Thursday with the RDA.'

Hugh had heard of the RDA—the Riding for the Disabled Association—a charity which with the help of volunteers and fundraisers offered an opportunity for disabled children and adults to ride carefully chosen ponies and horses. The Princess Royal was a great supporter of the organisation, he knew.

'Do you enjoy it?' he asked.

'Yeah.' There was an enthusiasm in his tone Hugh hadn't heard before, and he guessed this was one part of being disabled that Edward didn't find too irksome! 'Although,' he continued in his slow, careful speech, 'sometimes I'm not sure who's disabled, the ponies or the riders.'

Hugh laughed. 'Are the ponies all old crocks, then?'

'Not really. Some of them are quite young, but most of them have arthritis. There's one, Pipkin, who's new. He's only nine but he can't do much any more because of his leg. He's a lot like me. He'd like to do more—I can feel it in him. He was sort of boiling inside with enthusiasm, but his body just won't do it any more.'

'I guess you would identify with that,' Hugh said gently.

Edward gave a little snort. 'Just a bit. I get so sick of everyone thinking I'm thick, just because I talk slowly and can't move fast. People talk down to you—patronise you. It makes me mad. I get so frustrated.'

Hugh moved round to the other side of the treatment couch and spread some cream on Edward's back, then turned on the ultrasound machine and ran the head lightly over the area of his sacrum and lumbar spine.

'Do you get bullied much at school?' he asked casually.

Edward stiffened a little, and Hugh rested a warm hand on his hip and squeezed gently. 'Don't tense up. Just let the ultrasound do its work. Just breathe deeply and let go.'

Gradually the boy relaxed again.

Hugh tried a different tack. 'So, tell me again how you fell,' he said softly.

The silence was broken only by the ticking of the timer on the ultrasound machine. For a long time Hugh didn't think Edward was going to answer, then he drew in a shuddering breath and let it out.

'This kid tripped me up on the stairs. He's a new kid in my year. He's been gunning for me all week, trying to prove something to the others—make his place or something.' There was a wry chuckle. 'Big mistake. They're all used to me now, and they get a bit defensive. That's why I don't want to say anything. They'll trash him if they know.'

'They?'

'Al and his mates. He's my best friend. He's Jamaican—his kid sister Flora's got CP too. He gets really mad if anybody messes with me—makes the Mafia look like kindergarten. He'll get in trouble if he's caught sorting this kid. He's done it before for me.'

'And you think he would again?'

Edward snorted again. 'I know he would.'

'Perhaps you need to have a quiet word with the one who tripped you up—warn him off.'

'Yeah, right—like he'll really listen to me!'

'He might—it'd be worth a try if it'll keep your friend Al out of trouble.' Hugh put the ultrasound head down and, using his knuckles, kneaded gently into the taut muscles.

'That feels a little better. How does it feel from your side?'

'Easier. Thanks.'

'I won't manipulate it today—it's too fresh and fragile at the moment. What I want you to do is go home, ice-pack it three times a day for ten minutes and rest as much as possible. I'll see you again on Monday evening at the end of surgery so I can spend as long as I need without time restrictions. I think the diary's looking a bit hectic for early next week and I don't want to just cram you into a little slot. Can you manage to get dressed again?'

Edward gave him a withering look. 'I expect I'll cope.'

Hugh laughed softly. 'Often my patients need help. A bad back's a bad back, Edward. It would be silly to mess yours up even more and make it worse just for the sake of your fool pride, wouldn't it?' He winked. 'I'll send in your mother in a minute.'

He found Miss Wright—not Judith, he reminded himself—where he'd left her, staring out of the window at the front garden. She swung round as he came in, and he felt the now-familiar thunderbolt slam him in the mid-section.

* * *

At last! She was beginning to wonder if she'd ever see her son again. She found a smile. 'Hi. How is he?'

'Stiff, tender—he's got a partial subluxation of the lumbosacral joint, caused by his fall, and the spasm of his psoas muscles isn't helping him stand properly.'

'They give him trouble,' she said with a sigh. 'It's postural, and because of his spasticity.'

'Yes. Anyway, he should be a bit more comfortable now. I've told him to rest over the weekend and he needs some frozen peas on it three times a day for a few minutes. Put them in a plastic bag and tie them up, and wrap them in a teatowel so he doesn't get freezer burns. Just refreeze them after each session.'

She smiled again. 'We have a bag of peas on the go most of the time,' she told him softly. 'Injuries are no stranger to him. He often turns his ankles.'

'He would. It's unfortunate—'

A noise in the distance caught their attention and he lifted his head. 'Was that Edward? Did you hear him call?'

Judith shook her head. 'No—is it someone at the back? I thought I heard someone a moment ago.'

'Christine. Let me just check she's all right. Would you like to go and make sure your son's managing to dress himself, and then we'll make you an appointement for next week?'

He excused himself and went down the corridor. She was just crossing the hall when he came back, looking distinctly harrassed.

'Problems?' she said instantly, searching his face for clues.

He rammed his hands through his hair. 'You might say that. Miss Wright, have you ever delivered a baby before?'

Judith froze for a moment. A baby? Oh, Lord, no, don't

let her have to get involved with a delivery. Not after the disaster of Edward's birth. . .

'Well? Have you?'

'Only Woody,' she told him automatically.

His brow creased in puzzlement, but he moved on. 'I'll call an ambulance, but if you could go through there and talk to her? I think things are moving really very fast and she's a bit scared.'

She wasn't alone, Judith thought. She forced herself to walk down the corridor on legs like jelly. Please, God, don't let this be happening to me, she thought. Let him be wrong.

He wasn't. She found the woman lying on a comfy sofa, propped against one arm with her feet braced against the other—her face contorted with the effort of expulsion.

Judith didn't even have time to wash her hands, never mind make any kind of preparation for a sterile environment. She squeezed Christine's hand briefly, hitched up her dress and pulled down the tights and pants that the woman had tried—and failed—to remove. As Hugh came back into the room she was perched on the side of the sofa, the baby's head cradled in her hands, with no time to worry about her part in all this.

'Here,' Hugh murmured and, hitching Christine up a fraction, he slid a thick, soft towel under her, put his arm round her shoulders and let her hang onto his hand as the next contraction seized her in its grip.

'Aagh. . .' she groaned, tucking her chin down and straining.

Judith smiled at her. 'You're doing fine, Christine. Nice and gently. Just take it steady. Well done.' Heavens, was that her? She was talking on autopilot, functioning on two entirely different levels. God forbid that Christine should see the other level—she'd have hysterics!

Judith looked down at her hands. The baby's head lay there, streaked and smeared, the mass of dark hair pressed damply against the tiny skull. As Christine pushed the baby seemed to squirm and turn and twist in Judith's hands. Suddenly not only a head but a body lay there in her hands, tiny, dark red and utterly furious.

The blood-curdling yell was the most wonderful thing she had ever heard—second only to the siren of the ambulance which arrived at the same time, relieving her of the responsibility for the baby's welfare and any further part in its delivery.

'Thank God,' Hugh muttered beside her and, releasing Christine, he went to let them in. Judith lifted the baby up and laid him across Christine's now-soft abdomen. 'It's a boy,' she said, her voice choked with tears, and as the ambulancemen came in she went over to the sink, washing her hands as if she could take away the memory of the last wet, squalling newborn she had held.

His cry had been the same. Her joy in a new life had been the same. It was only later that she'd discovered how different he was to be. . .

Hugh appeared behind her, his hands cupping her shoulders with a gentle squeeze of support and thanks and all the other tumbling emotions childbirth brought kicking and screaming to the surface. 'All right?'

'Yes.' Surprisingly, her voice was steady. Now there's a miracle if you like, she thought. 'It's a boy,' she said unnecessarily.

'I know. Thanks for your help.'

She looked up at him, her eyes still misting with tears. 'It's all right,' she said, although it wasn't. Not for her—and not for Woody.

Hugh looked searchingly at her for a moment, then his hand came up and brushed her cheek. She was surprised to feel a tremor in his fingers. 'Do you want to go and make sure Woody's all right?' he suggested, as if he could read her mind. 'He may be a bit concerned.'

She nodded, smiled absently at the busy ambulancemen

and fled down the corridor. She arrived in the hall to find her son there with another woman behind him. She smiled at them both, a little stronger now she was away from the scene in the kitchen.

'No Christine?' the woman said.

'No—she's just had her baby—that's why the ambulance is here.'

'Here? She's had it here? Oh, how wonderful!' the woman exclaimed, obviously delighted. 'Everything all right?'

Judith forced a smile. 'Seems to be.' Funny, she couldn't share the woman's enthusiasm.

'Oh, do give her my best wishes. I'm Mrs Jennings, by the way. I'll go through and wait, shall I? Oh, how exciting!'

'Fine. Thank you.' She turned to Woody. 'OK, love?'

He nodded. 'Yeah—much better. I take it the receptionist had her baby just this minute?' he murmured.

She nodded. 'Yes, that's right. A boy. He looked so much like you—'

She broke off, unable to continue along that line of thought, but as usual Woody didn't miss a trick.

'Mum, it wasn't your fault,' he began, and then Hugh arrived.

'Sorry about that,' he said with a rather bemused smile. 'Babies have a way of arriving when it suits them. Um—let's have a look and see if we can make you an appointment for Monday, Edward—oh, excuse me—' He picked up the ringing phone. 'Good afternoon. Hugh Barber speaking. Can I help you?'

It took three tries before he managed to look at the appointment book without interruptions, by which time he was looked fairly ragged and Judith was wondering if they would ever get away.

'This is ridiculous,' he muttered when the phone disturbed them yet again. 'Let's ignore it.'

Judith reached out and covered his hand, stilling him
for a second. 'Can't you get her replacement in early?'

He snorted. 'What replacement? I'm so busy I haven't
even got round to advertising her post again yet. Finding
someone of the right calibre to handle confidential information is never easy, and the last crop of applicants was
dismal.' He snatched up the phone. 'Barber.'

A job. My God, she thought, it's a job, right here
in my lap!

'I could do it for you,' she offered quietly as he hung
up the phone. 'I've done a similar job before.'

He met her eyes, hope written ten feet tall all over his
face. 'Do you have the necessary skills?'

'I think so. I can type, answer the phone, organise filing
systems, use a computer or fax machine, do accounts,
keep records—'

'Stop! You're hired. When can you start?'

The phone, which had been briefly silent, rang again.

She smiled and reached for the receiver. 'How
about now?'

Hugh was so relieved that he didn't know whether to
laugh or cry. Since just after two, when Christine and her
baby had been handed over to the care of the hospital,
Woody had been ensconced in the snug in front of the
television, he had been seeing patients and Judith—well,
Judith had the place running like clockwork.

It had taken her about fifteen seconds to ask the questions she realised she needed to have answered, and after
following his patients out and explaining things to her a
time or two it dawned on him that his contribution was
entirely unnecessary.

She was a natural. She dealt easily with the patients,
she was warm and friendly but brisk enough to keep
things moving; she offered a choice of two appointment
times at the most, where the majority of people would

have asked when they would like to come and given
the patients enough rope to hang themselves. Not Judith.
'Monday?' she would say. 'Ten-thirty or twelve?'

And that was that.

She was wonderful. She was also very distracting. He
found himself thinking about her in entirely un-employer-
like terms and often, after seeing a patient out and
exchanging a few words with Judith, he would have to
drag himself away to the next patient, conscious of sport-
ing a silly grin but unable to do anything about it!

Damn, she made him feel good. He found himself humming at one point as he went into the kitchen in a lull to
tidy up after the pandemonium, only to find her in there,
too, having already done it. 'I was just going to bring
you a cup of tea,' she said with a smile, and left him in
there with it while she went to check Woody.

And Hugh, sitting down on the now-cushionless sofa
with his cup of tea, hummed cheerfully and thought that
life was pretty damn good. He'd solved his maternity
leave problem, Judith was employed and therefore able
to support herself and Woody, Christine had had a lovely
healthy baby and they had all survived the experience.
And he had managed to end up working alongside the
most attractive woman he had met in years.

Yup. Things were definitely looking up.

Judith couldn't believe her luck. She'd got a job! And
not just any old job, either. She was working with people
in a caring profession, which suited her much better than
being trapped alone in an office all day or stuck at a VDU
screen, tapping in numbers in a noisy, open-plan office
complex, and she was in such lovely surroundings, too.
From her position at the gorgeous antique desk she had
so much admired she could see out into the front garden,
which was a blaze of colour after the dry summer. The
recent rains had started everything off again and the

flowers were picking up, ready for the autumn flush. The roses were lovely, the Michaelmas daisies were just opening with brilliant spots of rich purply-blue against the green and the plants in pots and tubs around the door were full and lush and tumbling down towards the ground. Just sitting there looking at it all made her feel so much better.

To be paid for the privilege seemed almost superfluous.

As for the job itself, she was really enjoying it so far, and once Hugh had time to show her the ropes and introduce her to the computer system he used for patient records she could be of some real use in the little office behind his consulting room.

It was a pity she hadn't had time to grill Christine for some information, but she had no doubt that Hugh could fill her in. In the meantime she asked him if she had a query, dealt with the obvious and in the rare lulls she popped her head round the door of the snug and checked on Woody, lying stretched out on a big settee in front of the television fast asleep.

Thank God she would now be in a position to pay for his treatment!

It was a little after four when the peace and tranquillity of the big house came to a grinding halt. Utopia was shattered with the slamming of a door and the thunder of footsteps up the stairs behind her.

'Hi, Christine,' a voice yelled, and then the footsteps slowed, stopped and started down again in the other direction. Judith turned her head and found herself face to face with a boy of about Edward's age. And there, she thought wryly, the similarities ended.

He was a little taller, slim but muscular, and sported a superficial arrogance which she was sure was just a front. God forbid she should dare to mention such a thing, however! His mid-brown hair was just like his father's but a little darker, his features were a younger version as well but the eyes were startlingly and exactly the same vivid blue.

'Where's Christine?' he asked abruptly.

Judith blinked. 'In hospital. She's had her baby.'

'Blimey. That was quick. She was here this morning. Are you from the agency?'

'No. I'm the mother of a patient, but your father—I take it Mr Barber is your father?' she checked, just to be on the safe side. The boy gave a quick nod, and she continued, 'Your father offered me the job as I was here and available. Incidentally, if you go into the snug you'll meet my son, Edward. He's taking up rather a lot of your settee, I'm afraid, but he's messed his back up. That's why we were here.'

'Oh. Right.' The boy shoved a hand through his hair in a perfect reflection of his father's own gesture and turned on his heel. 'I'm going upstairs—Toots is in the kitchen. Keep an eye on her, could you?'

Toots? Who—or what—was Toots? And how was she supposed to keep an eye on her and watch the desk at the same time? Oh, well. She left the desk and went through to the kitchen. A little girl was in there, balanced on the edge of the worktop, rummaging in a cupboard. Judith didn't want to speak for fear of making her jump and lose her balance so she stood by the door and waited as the child prodded about amongst the tins and packets.

Finally she came out triumphantly with a packet of chocolate digestives clutched in her hand and jumped down onto the floor, the long fair hair which was escaping from a rather tired ponytail bouncing and swaying as she landed. Then she turned and caught sight of Judith, and instinctively and instantly hid the biscuits behind her back.

Then with a total absence of guile she looked straight at Judith with those astonishing blue eyes and said, 'Who are you?'

'My name's Judith. I'm the new receptionist.'

'Oh. Where's Christine?'

'She's had her baby.'

The child's head tilted slightly, and she suddenly looked a little fearful. 'Is she all right?'

Judith smiled and propped herself against the end of the sofa. 'Yes, she's fine. She's gone to hospital to rest for a day or so. She had a boy.'

The little nose curled. 'Yuck. Poor Christine.' She chewed her lip. 'She is alive, isn't she?'

What an odd question. 'Yes, darling, of course she's alive.'

'My mummy's dead,' she confided.

'I'm sorry,' Judith said gently, one of her questions answered. 'That must be hard. Do you miss her?'

'No. She died when I was born.' Which, Judith realised, explained the strange question. 'I'm seven,' Toots added inconsequentially. 'Have you got any children?'

'Yes, Edward. He's in the snug at the moment.'

'A boy?'

The child's disappointment was so obvious Judith almost laughed. 'I'm afraid so,' she said with a wry grin. 'He's a nice boy, though. You might surprise yourself and like him.' She looked at the hand still hidden behind the child's back.

'Are you Toots?'

The little nose curled again with delicate disdain. 'My real name's Alice.'

'Well, Alice, why don't I put the kettle on and make us all a cup of tea? Or you could have milk or orange squash or whatever you usually have, and we can all have some of those biscuits you've got there.'

The child pulled the biscuits out and looked at them as if she'd never seen them before in her life. 'These biscuits?' she said innocently.

Judith hid the smile. 'Mmm. Would that be a good idea?'

Alice looked at her with guileless blue eyes and smiled. 'OK. Has Daddy got many more patients tonight?'

'About three,' Judith told her, 'but I'm sure you won't have to wait that long to have a biscuit—'

'Hi, Toots, what're you up to, tinker?'

Alice threw herself across the room into her father's arms and hugged him. 'Hi, Daddy. I helped Judith find some biscuits for us all,' she lied, and gave him the benefit of her megawatt smile.

He melted like ice cream in the sun. 'Well, what a nice idea. Are we going to have tea? Can you manage to put the kettle on, Toots?'

'Course I can.'

Hugh looked at Judith. 'I've dealt with Mrs Fraser. Mr Parkin isn't here yet, but he's so often late I'm not surprised. How's it going?'

'Fine.' She smiled. 'Excellent, I think. I hope I haven't made any howlers.'

He grinned, shedding years in the process and doing her blood pressure irreparable harm. 'I doubt it. Look, I tell you what, why don't you and Woody stay for supper and let me go through the ropes with you so you're all ready for Monday?'

'Oh.' She smiled weakly, still busily in the grip of her heightened blood pressure. Supper? Was that such a good idea? Good grief, girl, get a grip, she told herself. It's hardly a date! 'That would be very sensible, but I'd hate you to go to any trouble—'

'That's OK. We'll get a pizza delivered—we often do. Housekeeping isn't my best thing. Then we can really concentrate.'

There was a crashing sound from the hall and the kitchen door was hurled back on its hinges. 'Anything to eat in this place? I'm starving.'

Hugh raised an eyebrow a fraction. 'Hello, Martin. Good day at school?'

'Passable. Can I have a sandwich—hey, Toots, where did you get the biscuits from?'

'I helped Judith—' She caught Judith's eye and amended, 'They were in the top cupboard.'

Judith gave an almost invisible wink of approval, and Alice grinned just a tiny bit. Good, Judith thought. She knows I don't approve, and she also knows I won't rat on her.

Martin was looking at the sofa as he ripped open the biscuit packet. 'Where are the cushions?' he asked curiously.

'In the garden, drying off. I washed them,' Judith explained.

'Why?' Alice asked, as if washing anything was a totally foreign idea.

'Because that's where Christine had her baby,' Hugh explained, 'and they got a little bit wet. You remember what I told you about babies in tummies being in a sort of paddling pool? Well, when the baby's born the paddling pool empties—'

'Oh, yuck, Dad, all over our sofa?' Martin said theatrically.

'It was the tiniest bit, and I did wash it well,' Judith hastened to reassure him.

'Even so,' he groaned.

Judith stifled a grin. Let Hugh deal with this one. She was on the point of escaping to the reception desk when there was a bump against the kitchen door and Woody entered in in his wheelchair.

He stopped abruptly as he saw the children, and Judith saw the familiar shutters come down over his features. He looked almost desperately at Judith. 'Are we going home soon?' he asked in his slow, rather fractured speech.

'No, not yet. Mr Barber's got a couple more patients to see, and then we're going to stay to supper so he and I can talk about the job.'

'Oh.' He looked a little uncomfortable with that.

'Is that a problem, darling?'

He shrugged. 'No, I suppose not. Is there a loo?'

'Yes, of course.' Hugh jumped to attention and turned to Martin. 'Marty, this is Edward Wright, Judith's son. He's in the same year as you at school. Woody, my son, Martin, and my daughter, Alice, better known as Toots. Marty, would you take Edward and show him where the cloakroom is, please?'

Judith looked at Martin to gauge his reaction, and her heart sank. He had that 'Oh, no, I'm going to have to talk to a cripple' look that so many people got with their first contact with Woody. Mutinous, slightly appalled, uneasy.

'I'll show him,' she said, starting forward.

'That's all right, Martin can manage. We've got patients to deal with. Marty, make a pot of tea for us all when you've done that, could you?' He took her arm and steered her up the hall, and as they turned the corner he said softly, 'Don't worry about him. He'll be fine.'

She chewed her lip. 'He hates meeting new people.'

'So does Martin. They'll be fine together. Ah, Mr Parkin, come on in. How've you been?'

'Funniest damn thing—got caught in the dog's lead and fell over and, d'you know, I do believe my back's been better ever since?'

Hugh laughed. 'You don't say? Come on in, let's have a look at this miracle cure.'

They were out ten minutes later, Mr Parkin looking as pleased as punch and Hugh looking slightly relieved.

'No charge, Judith. As the man says, he's cured. Give me a ring if you don't stay better, now.'

'Will do—thanks, Doc. I don't suppose you want to buy a dog—instant remedy?'

Hugh laughed. 'No, thanks—and I shouldn't go trying it again. You might not be so lucky next time.'

She watched him go and turned to Hugh with a smile. 'Cured by the dog, eh? That won't do your reputation any good!'

He chuckled. 'There ought to be a law against unlicensed practitioners.'

'Absolutely—especially the canine variety.'

He glanced at his watch. 'We've got a minute or two— let's grab a cuppa and some of those biscuits, if the kids haven't finished them all.'

They went back to the kitchen and found the three children in there, sitting round the table. The television was on in the corner but the atmosphere seemed tense. Superficially they looked like a bunch of kids watching the telly, but there was an uneasy and almost rebellious silence underlying the canned laughter on the programme.

She looked at her son and read the misery in his eyes, and turned to Hugh. 'Look, do you mind if I get Woody home to bed instead of hanging on after your last patient? He's had a long day and we've still got to do his physio before he can go to bed. Perhaps we could spend Monday lunchtime going through the job instead?'

He looked a little taken aback—and disappointed— but he disguised it quickly. 'No, of course not. Go now. I can manage. I wasn't really thinking. Sorry, Woody, is your back giving you stick?'

He dredged up a smile. 'I'll live. Thanks for my treatment.'

Hugh smiled wryly. 'You're welcome. I'm sorry I stole your mother from you at such short notice. Look, Judith, I tell you what—why don't you hang on half an hour until Mrs Radley's been and I'll run you both home?'

She chewed her lip again. 'Are you sure that's not a nuisance?'

'Of course it isn't. It's the least I can do—and, anyway, I really ought to pop down to the hospital and see Christine. I'll just go on from your place, then I'll get the kids a take-away on the way home.'

'OK.' What a relief, she thought, not to have to push the wheelchair round the corner and up the hill. It wasn't much of a hill but she wasn't much of a Mr Universe either, and she realised she was tired after her unexpected afternoon sloshing about in the deep end of her new job.

She swallowed her tea, took a bite of Woody's biscuit, squeezed him reassuringly on the shoulder and went back to the reception desk just as a young woman with a baby in her arms arrived.

'Oh. Christine's not here.'

'No, she's had her baby. I'm Judith, the new receptionist. Are you Mrs Radley?'

'Yes, that's right. Oh, how exciting. What did she have?'

'A boy—here, at lunchtime. It was all very quick and rather dramatic.'

'Really! What fun! Are they both OK?'

Judith shrugged and smiled, but the smile was a little forced. 'So far as we could tell,' she said, thinking of Edward and how normal and healthy he had seemed.

Mrs Radley looked down at the sleepy bundle in her arms. 'I brought Lucy in to show to her—I don't suppose you could hang on to her while I go in and see Hugh?'

Hugh appeared behind her and hijacked the baby. 'Hello, little one. My, what a lovely baby. Are you going to throw up on me?' he asked with tender teasing. Lucy blinked sleepily and her eyes drooped shut again.

'Dear me, I must be boring. Here you go, Judith— have a baby. Right, Jenny, how've you been? Any better?'

They disappeared, leaving her gazing transfixed at the

soft, downy cheeks of the tiny girl, her lashes faint crescents against the pale, blue-white skin. Her hair was fair, tiny soft wisps of it sticking up in little points, and it brought a lump to her throat. Two babies in one day. So many memories.

She bent her head and sniffed, and gave a ragged little sigh. She even smelled the same as Woody had. It had been such a happy time, for all the struggle it had been. Those few short halcyon months before she had realised anything was wrong held the most precious memories of her life.

She sniffed again, inhaling the soft scent of baby powder and ultra-fine skin, and sighed wistfully.

If only things had been different. . .

CHAPTER THREE

'NIGHT-night, sweetheart.' Hugh bent and kissed the soft little cheek, and smoothed the silky strands of hair back from his daughter's brow. 'I'll see you in the morning.'

'Night, Daddy,' she mumbled.

His hand was on the light switch when her voice stopped him. 'Daddy?' she whispered.

He paused. 'Yes, darling?'

'Did you see Christine, really?

'Yes—I told you all about it.'

'And was she really all right?'

His arm dropped back to his side and he went over to the bed again and perched on the edge. 'Toots, she's fine. She's just had a baby—that's why she's in hospital.'

'But my mummy died.'

So that was it. Hugh swallowed the lump in his throat and squeezed her little hand. 'I know, sweetheart, but your mummy was sick—her heart had a problem and she got suddenly much worse. Nobody could have prevented it.'

'Daddy?'

His heart sank. 'Yes, sweetheart?'

'If she hadn't had me, would she still be alive?'

It was a question he had asked himself over and over again, and he gave her the only answer he could—the one he gave himself. 'I don't know. I doubt it. I just know that part of her is alive in you, and if we hadn't had you then I would have lost that part, too, as well as all the rest of her. As it is, I've got a bit of her in Marty and a bit in you so I'll never really lose her completely. She'll always be with me, in a very special way, and she'll

41

always be with you because she's part of you.'

The little hand in his squeezed comfortingly. 'Do you still miss her, Daddy?'

'Yes,' he said quietly, his voice rough with emotion. 'Yes, Toots, I still miss her sometimes. I loved her very much.'

There was a thoughtful silence for a moment, then Alice said, 'Daddy, do you think you'll ever find another mummy for me? I think I'd like to have a mummy.'

Inexplicably he thought of Judith, and banished the thought as idle fantasy. He hardly knew the woman!

'Maybe, one day,' he replied.

'Then you wouldn't have to be so lonely any more.'

He bent and hugged her. 'I'm not lonely, Toots. I've got you and Martin to keep me company.'

Her little arms snaked around his neck and hugged him tight, and a wet and very welcome kiss landed somewhere between his eye and his ear. 'Love you, Daddy,' she whispered.

His throat almost closed up with emotion. 'Love you, too, Toots,' he whispered back, his voice strangled.

He kissed her again, tucked her up for the second time and turned down the light, leaving her door open a fraction so she didn't feel cut off.

Then he went back downstairs to the kitchen and made himself a cup of coffee while he got his mind back into order. Was he lonely? He'd assured Toots he wasn't, but of course he was—lonely for the company of a woman, a partner, a companion to share life's ups and downs. Still, as he'd told Toots, he had his children and so he was never really alone.

He could hear the television in the snug, which meant Martin was in there. He'd hardly seen him all week. Perhaps they'd have a game of chess. Humming softly, he ambled down the hall into the cosy room overlooking the garden, stretched out in the big comfy armchair and looked across at his son. 'OK?' he said with a smile.

'Mmm,' he replied, staring fixedly at the screen. He was sprawled on the sofa and hadn't even looked up as his father entered the room. Hugh flicked a glance at the apparently riveting television and saw some ghastly game show in progress.

Sighing inwardly, he girded his loins for confrontation and asked, 'Done your homework?'

Martin made an irritated clicking sound with his tongue. 'Dad, it's Friday.'

'Yes, and I'm sick of having every Sunday evening ruined by your homework because you've left it to the last minute.'

'I'll do it tomorrow.'

'Before or after you play squash with Colin or go to rugby club or any of the other distractions you'll find?'

'Before—for God's sake, Dad, what is this?'

'Watch your language, Martin—and what it is is me caring about you and your education.'

The boy gave a disgruntled sigh and turned his attention back to the set. His mouth was set in a mutinous line, but Hugh was too tired to deal with him tonight. He picked up the television remote control and changed channels.

'Hey! I was watching that!'

'"Was" being the operative word. Even if you're not doing your homework you are not watching mindless buffoons being cheered on by an audience of performing seals! You'll be brain-damaged by all these ghastly game shows.'

Martin sighed abruptly. 'Hardly—and talking of which, does Judith working for you mean we're going to have that spaz here all the time?'

Hugh froze, then very slowly pressed the off button on the remote. 'Spaz?' he said with deadly quiet.

Martin laughed awkwardly. 'Oh, come on, Dad, you know what I mean.'

'Yes, I do—unfortunately. I never imagined I would hear you say it, though.'

Martin squirmed, but he didn't back down. 'Dad, he's a spastic.'

'He has a condition known as cerebral palsy, which has affected the motor control part of his brain—'

'He's brain damaged.'

'Yes, he is—but please don't make the mistake of imagining he's stupid.'

'He speaks so slowly—it drives me mad,' Martin imitated so accurately that Hugh winced.

'It could have been you, son—or me, or your little sister. Especially your little sister, with the problems attending her birth. Just remember, until whatever happened went wrong Edward was all set to be a normal, healthy baby and grow up into a normal, healthy adult. He still is healthy, but because his muscles don't work quite as his brain would like to tell them to his body is in a weakened state. That in itself brings problems. Just imagine how you'd feel trapped inside an unco-operative body like Edward is.'

'Gross.' Martin shuddered eloquently. 'Does he go to that special school—you know, the one that has the mini-buses full of raspberry ripples?'

Hugh bit his tongue and refused to comment on the reference to cripples. 'No,' he said grimly, hanging onto his temper with difficulty, 'he goes to the school you'd be at if you weren't so disgustingly privileged and spoilt. Perhaps I should send you there after all. You might learn some manners and some human kindness.'

He stopped abruptly, jamming his hands through his hair and propping his elbows on his knees. His disappointment reflected in his voice, he added, 'It grieves me to say it, Martin, but there are times when I'm glad your mother isn't here any more so she doesn't have to see how badly I've failed in the way I've brought you up.' He looked up and speared his son with that searching cobalt stare. 'Where did I go wrong, Marty? Too hard? Too soft? Because as sure as hell I've done something wrong.'

Martin had the grace to blush and look uncomfortable. 'Ah, come on, Dad, don't get heavy with me. He's really hard work, you know?'

'He isn't. He's a good kid, struggling against enormous odds to cope in a world that just isn't geared up for anything but perfection. Normal, healthy girls get anorexia because the advertising industry tells them over and over again that the body beautiful is supposed to be scraggily thin and undernourished. Men have hair transplants and women dye their hair and have plastic surgery at huge expense because we can't cope with the natural consequences of ageing. Kids are committing suicide because they feel hopelessly inadequate because the world makes such huge demands on them. And you think it's too much trouble to talk to a very clever boy just because you have to wait a moment for his answers.'

'Dad, he's a dweeb—'

'And you're a disappointment to me, Martin.'

The boy shot out of the settee and glowered mutinously down at Hugh. 'I'm so sorry,' he said sarcastically, and flounced out of the room, banging the door shut so hard the frame shook.

'Martin!'

There was a pregnant pause, then the door opened again a crack.

'Slam that door once more and you're grounded for a month. Now go and do your homework, please.'

'Yes, sir,' Martin growled sarcastically. The door shut with a little less force, and Hugh closed his eyes and dropped his head back against the chair.

Where *had* he gone wrong? Had Martin always been like this? He didn't know. He'd been too busy working to notice. Had it been too much to expect that just knowing his father worked with disabled children would give Martin the same compassion and understanding?

Clearly.

Oh, damn. Hugh got up and rummaged in his CD collection, found something soothing and put it on. The lights were low, the music was soft and he found his thoughts turning yet again to Judith.

How difficult was it, bringing up a disabled child in this unforgiving world—never mind alone? He couldn't even manage a healthy, normal teenager. How Judith coped with Edward was a mystery. She must have to deal with all his frustration and disappointment, and probably her own guilt at her part in his disablement if it was due to a birth injury. Even if she hadn't been to blame, she would still blame herself. Parents always did, at least until they worked through that.

He wondered when she had found out there was something wrong. Had she known straight away? Unlikely, he thought, with that fairly low level of disability. Often CP was undiagnosed for months or even years. Had she had the support of her parents? A partner? Who was Edward's father? Did they see him?

So many questions—and none of the answers really any of his business. Only those relevant to his treatment of the child could possibly be considered justified, and yet he found the others clamoured at him.

Those questions and others—like how she would feel in his arms, and if her lips were really as soft as they looked, and if her body was as lush as it appeared or if the fullness of her breasts was just an illusion created by clever underwear.

He didn't think so. She didn't have the money for

clever underwear. So, real, then. Full and soft and womanly.

His body responded to the image with unbridled enthusiasm, and he groaned quietly and stared at the ceiling. Lord, it had been so long since he'd been with a woman. He'd gone a bit off the rails after Linda died, lost track of his moral judgement for a while. Then one night he'd looked at himself in a strange woman's mirror and hadn't liked what he'd seen.

He'd left without giving her an explanation, and he hadn't touched a woman since. In truth, he hadn't really wanted to, even then. He supposed he'd been trying to prove something to himself, drown his sorrows, hide from his grief. He'd never really enjoyed the company of the women he'd sought and used.

Now, though, he found he wanted a woman's company. Judith's, to be exact. And just to muddy the waters she was now his employee and the mother of one of his patients.

Great. Oh, well, there was no guarantee she'd be even slightly interested in him anyway.

Judith couldn't sleep. Woody, despite his long rest during the afternoon, was out for the count, wiped out by the pain and by the tiring start to the term, so she hadn't even had his company during the evening.

After his physio he'd gone straight to bed, and she'd been left staring blankly at some awful game show on the television. She'd channel-hopped for a while, but even her favourite forensic science mystery series had failed to hold her attention tonight.

She'd had a long, lazy soak in the bath—or she would have done if a strange restlessness hadn't possessed her so that she'd got the fidgets and had had to get out. She'd gone to bed with a book, got up again and made a cup of tea, then predictably had had to get up again to visit the bathroom.

By two she was no nearer sleep, and every time she lay down and closed her eyes she could see Hugh Barber's magnetic blue eyes and hear the deep, rich huskiness of his voice.

In her drowsy twilight state his voice said things to her that no man had ever said, beckoned her in ways no man had ever beckoned, so that her body ached and yearned for something she'd never known and yet longed for.

She turned over and thumped the pillow. How on earth was she supposed to work for the man if she went squishy inside every time he spoke to her? Damn him for being so horribly attractive. Quite apart from the eyes, which were enough to melt her in seconds flat, there was that incredible mouth—the lips firm, not too full but mobile, quick to smile and reveal sparkling, slightly uneven teeth. That little imperfection in an otherwise perfect face made him somehow more human and thus even more attractive.

She wondered how it would feel if he kissed her—and then told herself off for running away with adolescent fantasies. So he was drop-dead gorgeous. So what? He was also wealthy, successful and very, very eligible. He probably had a steady girlfriend, a discreet lover who knew the rules—or maybe a woman who featured very much in the lives of the children.

Damn. She punched the pillow again and rolled onto her back. That didn't help. Still she thought of him. Her errant mind conjured him out of thin air, brought him there to the intimacy of her bedroom. How would it feel, she wondered, to feel the warmth of his body against hers? To feel his weight pressing her down into the bed, the roughness of his hair against her tender skin, the sensation of his body intimately joined with hers—

No! She had to work for him! She couldn't let herself

think about things like that! She needed her job desperately—far too desperately to risk it on something as tenuous as an affair.

She didn't have affairs—and, anyway, even if she did there was no way he'd look at her. She was a frump—middle-aged before her time, sober and boringly serious and overweight and drastically in need of a haircut and a new wardrobe.

She laughed bitterly at herself for even daring to think of him in such intimate terms. Still, it was the closest she would ever get, and it was free.

She rolled to her side and curled up in a ball. It would be so nice, she thought sadly, just to have one night of wild passion with him. He was kind and considerate, thoughtful, understanding. Sensitive. She thought of the song about the lover with the slow hand and the easy touch. Oh, yes. She knew instinctively that he would be a good lover. It would be nice to experience that just once in her life.

She felt something wet run down into her hair, and then another, and another, dripping off her nose and splashing onto her hand.

She squeezed her eyes shut hard, pressing her lips together to hold in the sob. She was so lonely. Oh, yes, she had Woody, and she loved him dearly, but in the deepest part of her she was alone, empty. She always had been. Even with Mike, she had been alone. Perhaps especially with Mike. He'd only ever had time for himself.

Was Hugh lonely? His wife had died in tragic circumstances, if Toots was to be believed. Did he still grieve for her all these years later? Or was she just a distant memory now, too far away to keep him warm any longer?

Poor man. It must have been dreadful to lose her like that. Judith wondered if she had haemorrhaged. Probably. That was the most common cause of death in childbirth, she imagined. However had he coped?

'The same way you did,' she told herself. 'One day at a time. What else can you do?'

Nothing.

She was still doing it, getting through life one day at a time, living for Woody.

Would there ever be a time when she was living for herself? She thought of the future, with Woody grown up and living independently as she knew he would, and she felt a huge, bleak emptiness envelope her. . .

Monday was chaos. Organised chaos, with things running as smoothly as possible, but chaos for all that. A radiographer came in on Monday and Thursday mornings, she learned, and took pictures for Hugh in the little X-ray room, and on Tuesdays, of course, he had the children's clinic elsewhere. The X-ray room was used for traction at other times.

Patients for X-ray or traction had longer appointments which overlapped other patients', coming in a little before their time with Hugh either to be X-rayed or put in traction so they were ready for him at the right time. Those needing traction really needed to follow someone with a fairly simple problem, Hugh explained, so that he had time to nip out and set up the traction system during the preceding consultation. If that consultation was with someone who needed very intensive work there wasn't time to fit it in.

'How will I know?' she asked helplessly.

'Instinct.'

'What?'

'I'll tell you,' he relented. He grinned, and she melted inside.

'Don't tease me,' she scolded.

His grin widened. 'Why not? It's fun.' His eyes were warm, and she felt the sudden flutter of her heart against her ribs. Their eyes were locked, and time seemed to hang in the air, motionless.

Then he cleared his throat and looked away, and suddenly she could breathe again. 'Ah—um—that's it, really,' he said, and pushed his chair back and stood up, going round the desk to look out of the window.

The view was lovely, looking as it did down the garden, but there was not a lot happening out there. Nevertheless Hugh seemed to find it suddenly absorbing. Judith, utterly at a loss, stood up with her notebook.

'Um—right,' she said, grappling for common sense. 'Shall I make you a cup of tea before you have to start again?'

'Ah—coffee. Thanks. I'll come and get it.'

She left him, still staring out of the window in apparent fascination, and went into the kitchen next door—dropping her notebook on the table and sighing. 'Well, what on earth was that all about?' she asked the kettle. 'If I didn't know better I'd swear he was flirting with me for a moment there and then thought better of it.'

'He was.'

She dropped the kettle with a clatter and turned round, her hand over her heart.

'Don't creep up on me when I'm talking to myself!' she spluttered, blushing furiously.

Hugh smiled wryly. 'Sorry.' He looked down, drawing patterns on the kitchen table with his blunt fingertip. 'You were right. I was flirting with you, and I did think better of it. I'm sorry. I didn't mean to put you in a difficult position. It won't happen again, I promise.'

Judith was aware of an overwhelming sense of disappointment. She'd been right. He'd flirted by accident, just because he was an open, friendly sort of person, and she'd been silly and let herself get all flustered by it. It was meaningless, as natural to him as breathing, probably, and she had been foolish to read anything into it.

'Forget it. Don't apologise,' she muttered and, turning round, she picked up the kettle out of the bottom of the sink and filled it. 'Tea or coffee?'

'Coffee.' There was a silence, then he said very quietly, 'Judith?'

Slowly, her heart pounding, she turned round and met his eyes—trapped by the Mediterranean blue. 'Yes?' she said hesitantly.

'I'm sorry if I embarrassed you. It's been a long time since I've found any woman attractive. I think I've just forgotten how to behave, and it's all much more complicated with you working here.'

Oh, no, he's going to tell me he wants me to leave, she thought desperately. Oh, he can't. I need this job!

Something must have shown in her face because he stepped forward and cupped her shoulders with his warm, firm hands.

'What?' he pressed. 'What is it?'

'Can't we just work round it?' she asked, struggling for calm. 'If we pretend it never happened and start again, can't we just see if we can work it out? Hugh, I need this job—'

'Judith? I'm not suggesting you should leave! That's the last thing I want! I was just wondering if we could balance our working relationship around the way I feel, or if I'd blown things by getting interested.'

She blinked. 'Interested? You're interested—in me?'

He gave a surprised grunt of laughter. 'Well—yes. Isn't it obvious?'

She shook her head. 'No—not to me. I thought I'd imagined it or you'd flirted with me by accident.'

His grin was rueful. 'Unfortunately not. I haven't been able to think about anything but you all weekend,' he confessed wretchedly.

She laughed. She didn't mean to, but his discomfiture so exactly matched her own that she couldn't help herself.

'Oh, Hugh,' she said softly. 'I felt just the same.'

'You did?'

His hands left her shoulders and cupped her face. He was standing so close she could almost feel his heartbeat, and she wanted nothing more than to reach up and draw his face down and claim that kiss she'd been thinking about all weekend. Their eyes were locked, their chests rising and falling rapidly—their breath mingling in the narrowing gap between them as his head came down towards hers.

Then suddenly, without warning, he released her and stepped back, breathing harshly in the quiet kitchen.

'This is a lousy idea,' he muttered and, backing away, he turned on his heel and left the room.

Staggered by his sudden withdrawal, Judith sagged back against the worktop and laid her hand over her trembling mouth. Her lips were soft, full, aching expectantly for the kiss they had been denied, and her legs were like jelly. She felt as if she must be dreaming, going crazy. She'd imagined it! She must have done! Oh, how embarrassing! Had she really stood there, gazing up adoringly at him, and all but begged him to kiss her?

She closed her eyes and sighed.

What an idiot she was being. She was thirty—a grown woman! If a man who was free to do so wanted to kiss her why was it such a big deal?

Because it is for you, her mind replied. Men don't kiss you, Judith. You're a frump. You're boring. It doesn't happen.

Damn it.

She made the coffee and took it through to him. He was in his little office still, working at the desk. He glanced up briefly, thanked her for the coffee and handed her a sheet of paper.

'Could you type this out for me, please?' he asked. Oh, dear. Politely distant. So that was how it was going to be.

'Sure,' she agreed, and took it and went over to the other desk, the one with her computer on it. She was halfway through doing it when he stood up and went out.

'I'll let Mr Conway in. You carry on. I'd like that to go today, if possible.'

'Fine.'

She finished typing the letter onto the computer and printed it in between answering the phone to patients.

At three o'clock there was a phone call from the school to say that Woody's back was giving him a lot of pain and he was lying down in the sick room and could she go and fetch him?

Hugh came out of his surgery just as she took the call, and the look on her face must have alerted him.

'Problems?' he mouthed.

She nodded and asked the secretary to hang on. 'It's Woody. His back's bad. They want me to fetch him but I can only go on the bus—'

'Tell them to put him in a taxi and send him here.'

She felt her eyes widen. 'But, Hugh, I haven't got any money. I can't possibly afford to pay—'

'I'll pay for it. Just tell them to do it.'

So she made the call, wondering if she would be for ever in his debt or if she would actually earn any money over and above Woody's treatment and taxi fares by the end of the month. If she could even survive that long. There was precious little food in the house—

'What now?' he asked softly.

She looked up, surprised that he was still there—standing watching her thoughtfully as she chewed on her lip.

She let out a shaky sigh. 'Hugh, I don't know how we're going to survive. What with the taxi fares and Woody's treatment, there'll be nothing left of my salary—'

'What? I won't be charging you for Woody's treatments. I never charge to treat my employees or their

immediate families. One of the perks of the job. Didn't
I mention that?'

She searched his face for any hint that he was lying,
but he would have made a fine poker player.

'I hate charity,' she muttered. 'If it wasn't for
Woody—'

'Judith?'

'Mmm?'

'Shut up.'

She looked up again into his gently smiling eyes.
'But it's—'

'For Woody,' he finished. 'Let me help him, Judith. I
can do so much to relieve his spasticity and improve the
mobility of his joints. I want to do some cranial work on
him as well. I think it could really make a difference to
him. Please let me do it. Don't confuse things by getting
on your high horse and letting your pride get in the way.'

He was utterly sincere and he made her want to cry.
She swallowed, not only her pride but the huge lump in
her throat as well. 'Do you really think you can help him?'

Hugh nodded. 'I hope so. I'd really like to have a go,
anyway.'

She chewed her lip again. 'It just seems to be taking
advantage of you.'

'Nonsense.' He seemed fascinated by her mouth, and
she stopped nibbling it and straightened up. 'There's
another thing I've been meaning to discuss with you,' he
went on, dragging his eyes up from her mouth. 'I wondered how you would feel about perhaps helping out here
in the evening. You have to go home and cook, I have
to cook for the kids—they're tired and grotty by the time
I finish off and get a meal on the table. I wondered if it
mightn't help us both out if I buy the food and you cook
it and we all eat together at the end of the day.'

Now he wanted to feed them as well! Judith stiffened

and drew in a deep breath. 'Hugh, I don't need your charity—'

'Charity? What the hell are you talking about? I hate cooking! The kids hate my cooking. Even if you're a lousy cook it would at least be differently foul!' He perched on the edge of the desk and leant over her.

'Judith, believe me, it isn't charity. If you could throw a meal together during the last part of the afternoon, and supervise the kids with their homework while I treat the last few patients, it would make my life so much smoother. They might also stand a chance of growing up knowing that food didn't have to come out of a take-away or a TV dinner packet.'

Heavens, she thought, he was almost convincing. Not that she took much convincing. With no food in the house and no money to buy any, it was difficult to imagine how she was going to feed them both until the end of the month. It would save her a fortune, not only on ingredients but on electricity, on heating—in all ways. And, of course, it would mean Woody could come straight here after school and she wouldn't have to worry about him being at home on his own.

He must have seen her wavering because he reached over, brushed his knuckles against her cheek and said with a coaxing grin, 'Attagirl. Give it a try—perhaps a week or two. Say it's just until Edward's back's better, and we'll see how we all get on with the idea. OK? Then, if your cooking's worse than mine or you find you can't bear to cook for such fussy morons as us, we've all got a let-out clause.'

'Just a week?'

'Mmm—initially, if you like.'

'Hmm.'

'Hmm?'

'I'll think about it.'

He grinned and shrugged himself off the desk. 'I knew you'd agree.'

She closed her eyes and shook her head. She must be mad. Housekeeper as well as receptionist? And how would Woody feel? Oh, well, she could always change her mind. . .

CHAPTER FOUR

HUGH was feeling very smug. Not only had he got a very attractive and delightful woman working as his receptionist and secretary, she was going to cook for them as well. Brilliant, he thought. The kids would be happy, it would be one less worry on his plate, so to speak, and he would have Woody here on the spot to treat him for as long as it took.

Once he started treating him cranially he might find the treatments went on rather a long time because sometimes he got locked into a pattern of flow of the cerebrospinal fluid and there was nothing to do but go with it and work on it until the fluid was responding in the right way.

It was like a tide, the slow pulsing flow of liquid that bathed the brain and spinal cord, pumped by the subtle action of the skull bones and the tilt of the sacrum and creating a tidal effect that swept the fluid into all the nooks and crannies of the brain to bathe the outside with the nourishing broth. Any head injuries, spinal inequalities and inhibitions to normal healthy movement could cause eddies and swirls to form in the fluid, preventing cerebral sinuses from draining and leading to headaches, dullness, tiredness—the list was endless.

Properly functioning, the cranio-sacral rhythm kept the whole system healthy. Conversely, problems with it could affect any part of the body and slow down recovery or halt progress. Woody had enough problems without imbalances in his cranial system. If he could get those working properly, the boy would be more likely to achieve his potential.

He'd seen it happen with lots of kids at his children's clinic. So many of them were with him because nobody else had been able to do anything to help them, and then, of course, there was the tendency to say that because it had been going on for so long the problem had resolved itself spontaneously and it was nothing to do with his treatment!

If only he was the first port of call and not the last resort, he thought wearily, he could do so much more to help.

He glanced out of the window and saw a taxi pull up. Woody. Lord, he looked stiff and tense. Poor kid—

'You're very quiet today, Mr Barber.'

He glanced down at the smiling young woman on the treatment table. He had been giving her lumbar spine some ultrasound to improve the circulation to the inflamed tissues and help promote healing, and the steady ticking of the timer had sent him off into a daydream.

He smiled ruefully. 'Sorry. I've got a youngster just arriving for treatment that I've been a bit preoccupied with. There, that should make things a little easier.'

He put the head of the ultrasound down and, using his fingers, he massaged deep into the tight and tender muscles bracketing her spine. Yes, they felt easier. The whole area was moving much more fluidly now. He wiped away the last of the lubricant with a soft paper towel and wiped his hands.

'OK, let's have you sitting up. How does it feel?'

She moved much more freely, he thought, watching carefully as she swung her legs over the side of the table and sat up. 'Better. Oh, yes. Thank you.'

'Right. Well, take it easy this time. Don't lift anything heavier than a cup of tea for the next two days, and maybe this time you'll maintain the improvement.'

She laughed. 'Mr Barber, I'm a mother. I have two toddlers. You know that.'

He grinned. 'Yes, I do. Make them walk. Kneel down to help them onto the loo so you aren't bending over. Encourage them to be independent.'

She snorted. 'They need no encouragement. I spend most of my time lifting them down off the furniture!'

'Just do your best. Pop your clothes back on and I'll make you an appointment for ten days.'

He went out into the hall just as Judith came back out of the snug. She was looking worried, but her eyes lit up when she saw him and something odd happened inside his chest.

'How is he?' he asked, amazed his voice was so normal.

'Awful. He can hardly walk. He's on the sofa.'

'Right. I'll go and see him. Can you make Mrs Stafford an appointment for next Thursday, please?'

He went into the snug and perched on the coffee-table just near Woody's head. 'Hi. Rough day?'

The boy's smile was thin, and he looked close to tears. 'Yeah,' he muttered. 'Mum said the taxi was your idea. Thanks.'

'Any time. Let me give you a hand to get out of those things, and I'll have a go at you where you are. I think we need to get some anti-inflammatories into you, and I'll just do a little soft tissue work to help you relax a bit. Then I'll do some more later at the end of surgery when I've got more time. OK? And in the meantime you can rest.'

'OK. Thanks.'

Lord, he was thin, Hugh thought as he eased the trousers down Woody's wasted legs. Thin, tense and suffering. 'OK, that should do,' he murmured and, pulling his shirt up a little, he helped him roll onto his side. He was kneeling beside the sofa, not ideal but workable—just. At least he didn't have to bend.

He spent five minutes working into the muscles around the boy's pelvis and lumbar spine, then rolled him onto his back and tucking his fingers over the edge of the hip-bone, pressed down with Woody's leg bent at the knee and got him to slowly lower and stretch the leg down against the pressure.

The boy winced but said nothing as Hugh struggled to release the tension in the iliopsoas muscles that held Woody tipped forwards with his hips slightly flexed all the time. He repeated the exercise with the other leg, and was rewarded by an easing of the incredible tension in the muscle. Satisfied with what he had done so far, he helped Woody pull his trousers back up but left them unfastened for comfort.

'Right, I want you to lie on your back with this cushion under your knees, and try and get some sleep. I'll send your mother in with some pills, and I'll see you again in a while. There's a blanket here you can have over you. Would you like it?'

Woody nodded, and Hugh spread it carefully over him and tucked it in. Poor kid. He'd love just thirty seconds alone with the brat who'd tripped him up.

He went back out into the hall and was greeted by the slender curve of Judith's neck as she bent over the appointment book. Her hair was caught up in a bun, and the delicate arch seemed somehow vulnerable and unbelievably erotic. It's just a neck! he told himself. You treat necks all the time.

But it wasn't just a neck. It was Judith's neck, and he had a sudden and almost overwhelming need to lower his head and trail his lips over that soft, downy nape.

The phone rang and she picked it up, tipping her head sideways and then swivelling to meet his eyes. 'I'll just see if he's free to talk to you. Hold on, please, Mr Santos.'

She arched a brow and he shook his head frantically. The specialist equipment rep had been plaguing him recently, and Hugh was at his wit's end. Judith put the phone on hold and looked at him with a grin. 'What's it worth?' she murmured.

'Just get rid of him. I never want to see him again. He's extraordinarily persistent and he doesn't sell anything I'm interested in.'

She pressed the hold button again. 'Mr Santos? I've had a word with Mr Barber. He seems to think he's already explained to you that he doesn't need any further equipment at the moment. You have? Well, if you could send him a brochure he can contact you if he's interested. Well, when you do have the brochure, perhaps? Thank you so much. Goodbye!'

She put the phone down.

He grinned. 'I love you. That man is such a pain.'

Judith chuckled. 'He's sending you a new brochure when he gets one—there's all sorts of new stuff he's sure you'll be interested in.'

'In his dreams. They're far too expensive, and they offer lousy value for money. I don't mind spending it if I feel it's justified. Their stuff doesn't justify it.'

She leant back and eyed him curiously. 'So why does he keep pestering you?'

'Because I bought something two years ago to get rid of him.'

'Oh. Bad move.'

'Absolutely.' He exchanged a grin with her, trying to keep his eyes off the smooth, pale skin that disappeared into the open V of her blouse towards those lovely, real, womanly breasts. His hands ached to feel the weight of them, and with a muffled groan he turned towards his consulting room.

'You've got a new patient in there—Mr Harper? He says he's got a knee problem.'

Hugh nodded. 'Fine. Thanks. Could you take Woody in two ibuprofen out of the desk drawer—and if you've got ten seconds I'd love a cup of tea when I've finished with Mr Harper.' He took the new record card from Judith's outstretched hand, gave her a smile that he hoped didn't look as lustful as it probably did and went in to see his patient.

Perhaps this attraction that he felt for Judith was going to be a two-edged sword—and just at the moment it was threatening to run him through right where it hurt!

Judith went to see her son, found him already asleep and so left him. Rest would do him·as much good as pills, and he could always take them later.

She went into the kitchen, put the kettle on and decided to look in the freezer for something for supper. With Woody pinned out like a butterfly, tonight seemed as good a night as any to start their experiment, she thought, and so she ought to be giving the meal some consideration.

She went into the big utility room beyond the kitchen, lifted the lid on the chest freezer and stared at it in dismay.

Two little basic pizzas, a large leg of lamb which would simply never defrost and cook in time, half a dozen scrawny sausages and a packet of smoked salmon.

Wonderful. Apart from some frozen peas that looked as if they'd been used for an ice-pack, there was just the usual debris—lumps of ice, unidentifiable bits of meat, oven chips, peas and sweetcorn and little cardboard tabs off packets, two clothespegs, a broken rubber band and a refugee ice-lolly.

Wow.

Casserole? she thought with a chuckle. What about the fridge and cupboards?

They weren't much better, she discovered. Apart from some herbs and spices, all she could find in the cupboards were a tin of kidney beans, a tin of chick peas, two tins of tomatoes, half a packet of pasta twirls and a packet of instant mash. The fridge contained some tired cheese, several bottles of milk and a few shrivelled carrots.

Oh, well. She liked a challenge.

She found some onions and potatoes in a vegetable rack in the utility room as well, and with a sigh she assembled her ingredients, found a casserole dish and threw everything in. Kill or cure, she thought. It was almost certain to terminate their trial of her housekeeping skills at the first hurdle! Oh, well.

There was a little ting from the hall as the glass door opened, and she went back out to the reception desk, checked in the next patient and went back to the kitchen. The casserole was just starting to bubble, and to her utter amazement it smelt quite reasonable.

Wonders would never cease. She made the tea, left it poured in the kitchen and went back just as he came out. 'Your tea's in the kitchen,' she told him.

He grinned, blew her a kiss and disappeared down the corridor, oblivious to her jiggling heart. Damn him, why was he so—so—oh, whatever! He ruined her composure umpteen times a day with such casual ease! She was going to have to get a grip on herself.

She didn't have long to fret. Hugh's exit was closely followed by Mr Harper's.

'I need to come again in a week, he says,' the patient told her.

'Next Monday? Four-thirty suit you, Mr Harper?'

'That's fine. D'you know, he's amazing. They've been treating my knee and all the time it was my back, apparently. Isn't that incredible?' He waggled his fingers at her and walked out without a trace of a limp.

She smiled and went and found Hugh.

'Another satisfied customer.'

'Mmm. He fell on his knee and they kept treating it. Actually, it was referred pain from his sacroiliac joint. He must have unsettled it as he landed—all that push up through one side of his pelvis puts a lot of strain on the junction with the spine. It's not surprising, really. It's just surprising that nobody else thought of looking at his back.'

'Oh, well, he thinks you're wonderful. Definitely flavour of the month.'

'Talking of which, this smells really interesting. What on earth did you find to cook? We were down to empty plastic bags in the freezer, I thought.'

She chuckled. 'A few sausages, some tomatoes, carrots, potatoes, kidney beans, some herbs and spices—and I thought I'd cook the pasta and throw it in at the end.'

He laughed softly. 'You're amazing. Tonight, after I've finished treating Woody, I'm going to run you home and then go to the supermarket and buy some food. If you've got any preferences or want to have any input, can you give me a list before then? Otherwise you'll end up with a whole slather of incompatible ingredients and you'll hate me to bits.'

I doubt it, she thought, watching him down his tea and stride back down the corridor to his patient. It would take more than incompatible ingredients to make her hate him—much more.

She sniffed the casserole, smiled with satisfaction and topped up her tea. The phone was mercifully quiet for the first time that day, and the house was peaceful—

A door crashed and the peace was shattered.

'Hi—ugh, what's that weird smell?'

'Supper. Hello, Martin, hello, Alice. Had a good day?'

Alice came and stood right by her and opened her mouth, sticking a grubby finger in it. 'I ot a oose ooth,' she announced.

Judith gently extracted the finger from the mouth. 'Pardon?'

'I've got a loose tooth—look!' And she proudly wiggled it again.

'Wow. That's very loose.'

'Mmm. And when it comes out the tooth fairy will

come and take it away from under my pillow and give
me some money.'

Judith pretended amazement. 'Really?' she said with
wide eyes.

'Really—well, no, not really. It's Daddy, actually, but
he doesn't know I know. I do, though. It's good. The
more fuss I make the more the tooth fairy leaves.'

Crafty little minx, Judith thought affectionately.
'Woody always had a fixed rate. Ten pence for a front
tooth, twenty for a back one. One had to be taken out by
the dentist—I think that was fifty pence.'

Alice looked horrified. 'I get a pound for every tooth!
More if I really cry.'

'Yes, well, you shouldn't. It's not fair on Dad—it's
just using him,' Martin told her, propping his feet on the
table and looking expectantly at Judith. 'Any tea?'

Talking of using people! 'Yes—in the pot,' she told
him. 'Help yourself.'

After a second of shocked silence he dropped his feet
to the floor, shuffled over to the cupboard and
extracted a mug.

'Any biscuits?'

'No, you finished them on Friday—unless someone's
been shopping?'

Martin snorted. 'Fat chance.'

'Well, your father's going tonight,' she told him as she
headed for the door. 'Why don't you two write a list of
things you'd like him to get and then perhaps you can
have some snacks for when you get in from school? I'm
going to be cooking for you this week, anyway, while
Woody's off school. He's in the snug, by the way, on
the sofa.'

'Again?' Martin said, and Judith wondered if that was
real animosity in his voice or if she was just being hypersensitive. Oh, well. She went back to the office, scooped
up the record cards and began to file them. If Martin

really resented Woody then she would have to tell Hugh
they couldn't stay on at the end of the day and eat with
them. She could still cook, but she wasn't exposing
Woody to any unnecessary suffering—and if Martin was
feeling crowded in his own home that wasn't fair, either.

Oh, damn. Just when she thought her financial problems might be over. Oh, well, she'd just have to bite the
bullet and ask Hugh if he could pay her weekly at first,
just until she got on top of things again. She had three
pounds left in her purse to last till the end of the week,
and that was all. With the best will in the world there
was no way she was going to make it, even if she didn't
have to feed them in the evening. He could hardly be
expected to give them breakfast as well!

Hugh wrapped his hands lightly round Woody's head,
his fingers resting on the sutures or joins between the
skull bones. Closing his eyes, he allowed himself to tune
in to the subtle pulsing of the boy's cranial system.

Lord, it was soggy! Weak, very faint, sluggish—like
thick oil instead of thin, dragging its way round his brain.
Using gentle movements only, he exaggerated the movements—building up the swell like sloshing bathwater in
the tub. By working with it and not against it, the power
of the flow could be increased, but he had made sure
Judith knew he mustn't be interrupted because taking
his hands off Woody's head and leaving him with such
turbulence and power would be dangerous.

Once it was flowing well he could slow it down again,
settle it back into a natural, healthy rhythm which would
hopefully be maintained for increasingly longer periods.

For now, though, he closed his mind to everything else
and concentrated on the sensations his trained hands were
picking up. Yes, that was better. Oh, it was a joy to feel
how easily he responded. He could feel the bones locking
on one side, and a spiralling turbulence like a whirlpool

pulling him down in the same area—a sort of vortex in the fluid, interfering with the natural ebb and flow and compromising the action of the whole system.

If he could just free those bones, where the sphenoid joined the temporal bone—he must ask Judith if she had had forceps or a ventouse extraction when she'd delivered him. He had meant to ask today but there didn't seem to have been any time. Perhaps after supper—assuming Martin managed to swallow his animosity and be pleasant to Edward.

No. He wouldn't think about that—not about anything. Only feel. Yes. That was better. His fingers shifted slightly—holding, squeezing gently, so gently—and, yes, it freed a little, the vortex softening.

'How does that feel?' he asked the boy.

'Weird,' he replied, his voice drowsy. 'Sort of slippery. I can feel pins and needles—tingling, really—up and down my back and all round my head, especially where your hands are now.'

'Do you get headaches here?'

'Mmm—thin, sharp ones, like needles.'

'Yes. The bones aren't moving very well. Still, I think I should be able to sort it out a bit with time.' He settled the rhythm down, happy that the flow was brisker and more ordered than before, and then removed his hands.

'How does that feel?'

'OK.'

'Not light-headed or dizzy? No headache?'

Woody shook his head. 'No. It's fine.'

'Good. Do you want to come through to the kitchen and eat, or do you think you'd be better lying down?'

'I can sit,' Woody said, gritting his teeth as Hugh helped him up.

'OK. Come on through—I'll go and tell Judith we're ready.'

He left the boy dressing himself again and went into

the kitchen. There he found Martin sprawled on the sofa with his feet up, Judith at the table with Toots, looking at a reading book, and the casserole nowhere to be seen.

She looked up as he went in and smiled brightly. 'All done?'

Hugh nodded, fascinated by the faint run of colour as she looked at him. 'Yes. He's on his way.'

'I'll dish up, then. Alice, put your book away for now, darling. Martin? Could you lay the table, please?'

Martin gave her a fulminating look but dropped his feet to the floor and slouched over to the cutlery drawer.

'Forks?' he said economically.

'And knives, and spoons.'

'Spoons?' Hugh said, surprised. 'Why do we need spoons?'

'Because I found some apples on a tree in the garden and Alice and I have made an apple pie.'

Apple pie. Lord, he hadn't had home-made apple pie since Linda died. His mouth watered and he swallowed hard. 'Wow,' he said and almost kicked himself for sounding so inane. Still—apple pie?

The food was surprisingly good, considering the dearth of ingredients. Even Alice, fussy in the extreme, ate most of her little helping. Martin would have had more and so would Hugh, but there wasn't any so they had to content themselves with the pie.

And how. It was huge—deep and full of crunchy, tangy apple, the pastry thick and sweet and utterly wonderful. It would have been better with cream, but there wasn't any, of course, and Judith had made some custard which was nearly as good.

Sated, Hugh pushed away his plate and congratulated himself on finding such a treasure. He must look after her and make sure he didn't lose her—and, frustrating though it might be, that probably meant keeping his hands and his innuendo to himself and leaving her severely alone.

Oh, well, a man couldn't have everything, and nine out of ten was pretty damn good. . .

CHAPTER FIVE

JUDITH felt restless and disillusioned. Silly, really. Her life was wonderful at the moment. She had a job, Woody's back was making excellent progress, he was sleeping better, he seemed brighter and more cheerful and—unless she was imagining it—his speech was a little clearer, too. They were fed—wonderfully well, thanks to Hugh's shopping trips and generous provision. For the first time in years she had some real security, and yet she felt dissatisfied.

Absurd. How silly could she get?

It was Hugh's fault, of course. Ever since that first Monday when he had almost kissed her—unless she'd imagined it—he had been circumspect in the exteme.

Damn it.

No, that was stupid. It was better this way, with a little distance between them. Much more sensible. Very wise. Commendable.

She didn't want to be commendable. She wanted to be swept off her feet, kissed senseless—cherished. Oh, Lord, yes. Cherished.

A lump formed in her throat. She'd never been cherished. Not as a woman, as a lover. Not once in all her thirty years had a man looked at her with longing.

She didn't count Mike. He had been a boy, anyway, only nineteen himself, and he'd only taken what she'd thrown at him. Hugh, though—Hugh was a man, and in those few short hours before he'd put the brakes on, he'd looked at her with longing.

Would he cherish her?

Her eyes filled and she blinked.

What stupid, romantic nonsense! She was working for him. Of course he cherished her—as a receptionist, as a secretary, as a housekeeper, even. But as a woman?

No. Of course not. She was plain and frumpy and her clothes were the pits—

'Judith?'

She lifted her head, aware of a throbbing ache behind her temples. 'Yes?'

Hugh's brows quirked together and he studied her with those piercing blue eyes. 'Are you all right?'

She nodded, and winced. 'Yes. I just slept awkwardly—I've got a bit of a headache. What can I do for you?'

He was still looking at her, and she could have sworn something flickered in the back of those damnable eyes. 'Mr Harding wants another appointment in a week—book him in for traction, could you?'

She nodded, flicked through the appointment book to the following Thursday and frowned. 'It looks a bit busy. How about the morning?'

'No, it's in use for X-rays. Friday morning—here, after Mrs Jennings. She's usually quite straightforward. And when you've done that, can you come through to the consulting room?'

'Sure.' She smiled up at Mr Harding. 'Ten o'clock on Friday,' she told him, and wrote it on a card. As he left she glanced at the appointment book. Lunchtime, and the first afternoon patient had just cancelled so they had a long break. Thank goodness. She could take an aspirin and crawl into a corner for a while. Hugh usually left her alone at lunchtime, disappearing into his office and tackling paperwork after they'd shared a quick snack. It gave her nearly an hour, and today she would have even longer.

Unless whatever he wanted her for took a long time.

She went through into the consulting room and found

him standing at the window, his white coat undone and his hands thrust into his trouser pockets. He looked professional and masculine and utterly desirable, and she had to suck in a lungful of air to steady herself.

'You wanted me?' she said.

He turned his head slowly, and for a second or two she thought something burned like a flame in the depths of his eyes. Then his expression became neutral again, that brooding masculinity banished, and the professional man firmly back in place.

'You've got a headache.'

She blinked. 'Just a little one.'

'Let me have a look at you.'

'Me?' she all but squeaked. Take her clothes off in front of him? She'd rather *die* of her headache.

'Yes—come on, I don't bite. Just lie down on your back and let me see what's going on in there.'

'Like this?' she asked warily. 'I don't have to undress?'

'What's the matter? Afraid I'll jump on you?' he teased.

No. Afraid that, having seen her, he wouldn't want to was nearer the mark. 'Don't be silly. I just thought if anyone came to the door—'

'I could answer it. Anyway, it's irrelevant. You're fine like that. Come on, lie down.'

So she lay down, and his hands, firm and strong and gentle, wrapped around her neck and eased and pulled and stroked and stretched while he tutted and told her off for not mentioning it earlier. Then he grasped her head firmly in his hands, manoeuvred it into the right position and gave a little sharp twist.

So easy. There was a clunk from just below her skull and her headache vanished. His hands became gentle again, soothing and stroking her neck. His fingers tested the movement of the joints in turn, rocking and wiggling her neck while she lay there and thought she could tolerate a whole lot more of this.

Then he released her and stood up, helped her off the couch and grinned. 'Better?'

She smiled up at him a little warily. 'Thanks. Yes, it is, much better.'

'And I didn't attack you.'

She laughed softly. 'No, you didn't,' she replied, and was conscious of a little flicker of disappointment. How silly. 'Lunch?' she suggested, changing the subject rapidly before she got sucked into a discussion she didn't want to have.

'Wonderful. I'll be through in a minute.'

They had cheese on toast, nothing too thrilling but quick and simple. Then he sent her to lie down in the snug and rest her neck while he put the plates in the dishwasher and made some coffee.

She went, conscious of feeling a little achy, and lay self-consciously on the sofa. Moments later Hugh came into the room, put the mugs on the coffee table and looked down at her quizzically.

'OK?'

She laughed bitterly. 'Oh, yes. Apart from being a burden. I must say I've hardly been an asset to your practice. If it isn't Woody stretched out here wasting space and taking up your time, it's me—'

He sat, nudging her hip out of the way with his, and took her hands. 'What are you talking about, woman?' he murmured softly. 'You've been a huge asset to the practice from the moment you walked through the door. You've taken over Christine's job without a hiccup, you're feeding us the most superb meals, the kids are looking forward to coming home—and I look forward to getting up in the morning because I know you're going to be here.'

She blinked. 'Really?' she whispered.

'Really.'

Their eyes locked, his like blue lasers burning through to her soul. Then, inch by inch, his head lowered and his mouth touched hers.

Soft. So soft, so tender, so fleeting. He lifted his head and met her eyes again, and then with a muffled groan he shut them and his mouth found hers again. It was different this time, quite different. His mouth was hungry on hers—searching, seeking, demanding—and she, helpless, surrendered to his demands.

She felt the trace of his tongue along the seam of her lips and parted them as naturally as breathing, and for the first time in her life she felt the full power of a man's kiss.

Her heart bucked in her chest, her arms came up and snaked round his neck, holding him down against her, and then suddenly he was stretched out full length beside her—his body locked intimately against hers—and all she could think about was tearing his clothes off and feeling his skin against hers.

Until she felt his palm cup her breast. Then heat shot through her and she forgot to think, forgot to reason— forgot everything except clinging to him and letting him touch her with those unbelievable hands.

After an age he lifted his head and looked down at her. 'This is a lousy idea,' he whispered huskily.

She disagreed. His body felt good against hers—so good. He was hard and lean and needy, patently aroused, and she was responsible. That was the most powerful aphrodisiac in the world.

She touched his face, her hand trembling, and smiled tentatively. 'Actually, I thought it was rather nice.'

He grinned. 'You're right. I've changed my mind, I think it's a wonderful idea. Why don't we do it again?'

He swooped down again, trapping her face between his hands and steadying it as he kissed her nearly senseless. He only broke the kiss what seemed like aeons later so they didn't suffocate, and rested his forehead against hers while they both fought for breath and their hearts stopped hammering nineteen to the dozen.

He lifted his head and smiled, then his knuckles swept down over her cheek and she turned her head and pressed her lips to his hand. His thumb grazed her bottom lip, dragging it gently, and he groaned and dropped his head to the cushions beside her.

'Hell's teeth,' he muttered. 'That was meant to be a little peck.'

She chuckled, a little bubble of laughter rising up in her and welling over, and he hugged her gently and then disentangled his legs and swung them over the side of the settee.

'Here,' he said, offering her a mug. 'Sit up and drink this before I do away with your virtue altogether.'

Her laughter died. 'Hugh, I don't have any virtue,' she said flatly. 'I'm an unmarried mother. My parents threw me out, my friends didn't want to know me. If you're worried about my virtue you're about fifteen years too late.'

'Tell me,' he instructed, his voice gruffly gentle, and because she needed to explain herself to him—because she had to be honest and let him know what he was getting into—she told him.

'I was fifteen and a half. I'd met this musician at a dance I'd gone to with some friends. His name was Mike, and I thought he was wonderful. He lived fairly locally, and he asked if he could see me. It took about a week before I was running around with the wrong crowd, smoking, drinking, laughing too much—you know the sort of thing. I thought he was the best, the funniest person I'd ever met, and I was totally committed in no time flat.'

'What did your parents say?'

She laughed softly. 'My parents didn't know a thing

about him. They wouldn't have approved. I lied to them endlessly, and they were too busy to smell a rat. They had a hectic social life and most of the time they didn't even know if I was in or out. Anyway, to cut a long story short I became pregnant, and the second I was sixteen they threw me out.

'I went and lived with him in his squat, and I discovered he was morose, footloose—just an aimless drifter. We went on the road with his band in a terrible beat-up old van, and we ended up in Scotland. A friend lived on a deserted island in a croft. We were going to stay with him.'

She fell silent, remembering her first sight of the croft, and a shudder ran through her.

'Tell me about it,' he prompted softly.

She sighed and shrugged eloquently. 'The roof was full of holes, the windows were gone, the floor was bare earth. We were camping out, it was October and I was seven months pregnant. It rained almost constantly, and I wanted to go back. Mike promised we'd only stay one more night and they opened a bottle of Scotch, and then another, and then someone produced some drugs. In the middle of it all I went into labour.'

'Oh, hell.'

'Yes. I had Woody on my own, with the others passed out all around me and the rain coming through the roof and nobody to get help. He was born on a beautiful morning as the sun came up, and he was the most wonderful thing I'd ever touched in my life, but having him had nearly killed me and, as it turned out, it had nearly killed him, too.'

His thumb brushed her cheek and she realised she was crying, great wet tears streaming down her cheeks.

He said nothing, just turned her into his arms and cradled her head against his shoulder and held her while she cried. When the tears slowed and hiccupped to a halt he shoved a tissue into her hand and smoothed her hair and waited for her to gather herself together.

'When did you know he had problems?' he asked gently when she was more or less in one piece again.

'Six months later? Maybe a little more. I'd gone home to my parents and they'd turned me away, and Social Services had found me a place in a hostel. It was my health visitor who finally agreed with me that there was something wrong. I just knew there was, but I wondered if I wasn't inventing things to flagellate myself with. I contacted my parents but still they refused to help. I haven't spoken to them since.'

'How about brothers or sisters?'

She shook her head. 'No. I was an only child—an accident. They never intended to have me, and I think they were a little embarrassed at being caught out. I interfered with their plans, with their careers, with their social life. They were typical middle-class intellectual snobs, and when I disgraced them they just couldn't handle it. I understood that—'

'What? You're defending them?' Hugh looked outraged. 'For God's sake, Judith, you were a child! You needed help and support, not condemnation! What were they thinking of?'

She gave a wry smile. 'Themselves, of course. What else would they think of?'

Hugh muttered something unprintable and hugged her again. She rested her head on his shoulder and decided she could get quite used to it. She'd had the urge to do this since the first time she'd met him, and it was such a relief to do it now. He was just so solid and comforting and undemanding—well, that wasn't really true. When he'd been kissing her he'd been quite demanding, but he'd given far more than he'd taken—far more than he could ever realise.

He'd given her confidence in herself as a woman, and now with his understanding he'd given her back some of her self-respect. Not all. She didn't feel she deserved it all back because she'd been very foolish and that sort of foolishness deserved to be remembered.

Maybe if he spent a lifetime telling her. . .

A lifetime? What was she thinking about? She was his receptionist—she was covering maternity leave, for heaven's sake! It wasn't even a permanent job! She pushed him away and struggled up so that her feet were tucked under her bottom.

'Coffee?' she said a little hoarsely, and he passed her the tepid mug and she sipped it, curling her nose up. 'Yuck. I'll make some more.' She wriggled off the settee and took Hugh's mug, then padded barefoot into the kitchen.

He followed her, took the mugs out of her hands and turned her back into his arms. 'Forget the coffee,' he murmured, and then his lips were on hers again and the world was spinning on a different axis, and she really felt that if he let her go she'd fall flat on her face.

It was the phone that brought them to their senses as it shrilled in the silent house, shattering the tension and dispelling the mood like mist in the sunshine. She went out to the hall and picked up the receiver, to find a patient on the other end of the line desperate for an appointment as soon as possible.

'He's got a cancellation at two—that's only ten minutes. Can you get here in time?' she asked.

'I'll do my best,' the patient told her, and rang off.

So much for their extended lunchbreak, but the way things were going, she had a feeling it was just as well. Hugh didn't seem in the slightest bit inclined to put on the brakes and she didn't seem to be able to. Someone had to, though, because she wasn't going to get swept away again on a tide of hormones and hero-worship.

Once in any girl's life was quite enough!

It was the longest afternoon of Hugh's life. All he wanted
to do was sit down quietly and think through what Judith
had told him, but instead he had an endless stream of
patients, followed by another confrontation with Martin
about homework—and then Alice had a screaming fit
about having her hair washed and wriggled about until
she'd got soap in her eyes and really had something to
scream about.

By the time he'd got her eyes rinsed out and the sham-
poo out of her hair and dried her and tucked her up in
bed he was exhausted. There was no two ways about it—
being a single parent was hell. At least with two of you
the problems could be shared.

He opened a bottle of wine, sat down at the kitchen
table and thought about Linda. At least he tried to but
the only face he could see was Judith's, the only voice
he could hear was Judith's, the only body he could
remember was Judith's.

He closed his eyes and groaned. He was getting
obsessed. Kissing her had been a big mistake. She wasn't
a woman a man could play with and then discard—her
life had been too full of rejection and indifference already.
No. If he was going to get involved with Judith he had
to be damn sure he wasn't doing it for the wrong reason—
and her soft, luscious, feminine body was definitely the
wrong reason.

Martin came into the kitchen in his usual flamboyant
style, crashing the door back on its hinges and dropping
into a chair opposite Hugh. 'I've done it,' he said
defiantly, 'so don't ask.'

'Good.' Hugh leant back in the chair and held the wine
up to the light, swirling the rich burgundy liquid and

watching the light splinter like rubies. 'Fancy a game of chess?'

Martin picked up the bottle of wine, inspected the level and agreed. Hugh gave a silent huff of laughter. Martin didn't have to worry about the amount of wine he'd had. That kiss had been enough to scramble his brains. The wine was just putting the finishing touches to his dementia.

They set up the board on the kitchen table and Hugh settled back and waited for his son to beat him. He didn't normally, but tonight Hugh felt just addled enough that it was a possibility.

He was right. Whether it was the wine or the thought of Judith, he found it impossible to concentrate and Martin had him thrashed in ten moves.

'Another game?' his son asked, grinning broadly.

'I don't think so. My ego can't take it. You ought to play with Woody, though. He's the school chess champion. He'd give you a run for your money.'

'Woody?' Martin's voice echoed his disbelief.

'So I understand.'

Martin looked a little stunned as he put the pieces away. 'Fancy watching some telly?' he suggested.

Hugh looked at his watch. 'Shouldn't you be in bed now?'

'Aw, Dad, come on. We never seem to spend any time together these days—especially now Punch and Judy are here every day after school.'

'Punch and Judy?' he repeated, his brows twitching together.

Martin grinned. 'Yeah. Toots thought that one up. It's her name for them.'

Hugh sighed and tunnelled his fingers through his hair. Kids. 'Are you and Woody getting on any better now?' he asked.

Martin shrugged. 'So-so. We ignore each other mostly. Seems to work. Toots likes him.'

Toots would. She liked everybody, but that was her mother in her. Linda had always had time for everyone.

He felt a sudden pang of guilt that he could have forgotten Linda when he'd loved her so much. She had been so important to him, her death so shattering, that he'd thought at first he'd never get over her.

Now he couldn't even remember her face, or the sound of her voice, or the feel of her body beneath his—

'Dad?'

He blinked and looked up at his son, heat crawling up his neck. 'Yes?'

'I said, are you coming in the snug?'

'Ah—yeah, sure. I'll be with you in a minute.'

He put the wine away, made a pot of tea and took it through to the snug. Even if it's a game show, he promised himself, I won't fight with Marty. We'll just sit and watch and chat and share the evening. Be friends. I mustn't lose touch with him like Judith did with her parents.

But it wasn't a game show—it was a documentary and they talked about the issues raised and Hugh was proud of his son. He didn't agree with him, but that wasn't the point. He was forming opinions, thinking about issues, growing up.

And when he's grown and gone, what then? he thought as he got into bed. Another ten, fifteen, twenty years alone?

His arms felt empty. He lay on his back, staring at the ceiling in the watery moonlight, and thought of Judith. Were they going to be lovers?

Somehow he thought so, but the more he considered it the more he thought it was a lousy idea. There were too many variables with the children involved—too many things that could go wrong, too many people to be hurt.

Even so, as lousy ideas went it still had considerable appeal. . .

Judith thought she must have been out of her mind. Fancy lying there on the settee and allowing Hugh to kiss her like that! Encouraging him, even! Lord, she must be crazy. She didn't do that sort of thing, didn't come on to men like that. Mike was the first and last man she had slept with, and she hadn't seen him for twelve years.

Woody didn't interest him. The thought of having a handicapped child was more than he could handle, and he now lived in America with his wife and two children and worked as a session musician for a recording company.

There had been no one since—and until today, really, she hadn't minded. OK, she was lonely, but the physical side of things hadn't bothered her. Not until she'd met Hugh, and even then it was only after he'd actually kissed her that it had hit her what she might have been missing. Today, when his lips had brushed hers like the touch of an angel's wing and she'd caught fire. Even the thought was enough to make her burn and ache for him.

She turned her face into the pillow and moaned softly with frustration. Somehow she would have to convince him to leave her alone, and she didn't have the slightest clue how she was going to do it because there was no way she could look him in the eye and tell him she didn't want his touch.

She was longing for it, aching for it, dying for it. Like a cactus in the desert, she had felt his touch like the kiss of rain and her heart had burst into blossom where before there had been an arid nothingness.

Yet it was too much, this wild blooming in the midst of nowhere, because like the desert flower it would be gone in an instant, over before she could draw her breath, and like the desert rain Hugh would move on without a backward glance and leave her withered in the dust.

Would it be worth it, though? That one flower in the desert, for all its fleetingness, had a beauty beyond price. She could treasure the memory in the long and lonely years when it was over—because over it would be. She knew she didn't have the attributes necessary to keep a man like Hugh interested for long.

She was convinced that his only interest in her was her convenience. She was there, available, and gazing at him adoringly every time he turned round. Of course he'd taken advantage of the situation. What normal man wouldn't?

But in the meantime, while he was interested, would it be so very wrong to indulge in a discreet little affair?

Foolish, yes, but wrong? She didn't think so.

No. It was nuts. She must be crazy even to consider it.

She thumped the pillow again and pulled it down into her neck. It was feeling a little fragile after her treatment, although the headache was gone. She turned over again, thumped the pillow into shape once more and promised herself a new one with her next pay cheque. That would be tomorrow. Good. It would serve to remind her that she had a working relationship with Hugh and not a social one.

The phone was relentless. That in itself was enough to remind her why she was in Hugh's house. One call was from Mr Parkin, the man who had tripped over his dog and cured his own back.

'I've done something rather foolish, m'dear,' he told her. 'I had to move some rubbish in the garden, and instead of doing it bit by bit I bagged it all up and tried to lift it into the car—and oh, I can't tell you how bad I feel. It's much worse than usual—aches like the dickens. I don't suppose there's a chance Mr Barber could fit me in, is there?'

Judith looked through the appointment book, but it was chock-a-block. 'I will ask him, but I don't think it looks like we've got anything today at all, Mr Parkin. Can I ring you back in a moment?'

'Yes, of course—and, please, m'dear, do your best, won't you?'

'Of course,' she assured him, and the first chance she had she collared Hugh. 'Mr Parkin—he's lifted some bags of garden waste and put his back out. Can you fit him in?'

Hugh sighed and shoved his hand through his hair. It was already dishevelled. It had been that sort of morning.

'I could fit him in here between Mrs Widdows and Dr Knights. She's usually quick and he's turned his ankle playing squash and shouldn't need long. We'll squeeze him in.'

'So, Mr Parkin, decided to go for the traditional remedy this time, have you, and not fall over the dog as a cure?'

The man gave a weary chuckle. 'Don't think I'll be trying that again in a hurry,' he said.

'Right, where does it hurt this time?' Hugh asked.

'Just here,' he replied, indicating a line down the centre of his back over his lumbar spine. 'It's not catching like it usually does, just aching and sort of throbbing.'

Hugh frowned slightly. Throbbing? 'Let's have a look at you, then,' he said. 'Could you lie on your right side facing me?'

Hugh stood beside the treatment table, looking down at Mr Parkin as he drew his legs up, and then he paused.

Yes, there it was, a definite pulsation in the abdomen. Gently, very carefully, he eased the legs back down. 'Would you roll onto your back for me, Mr Parkin?' he asked. 'I just want to have a look at your tummy.'

'Thought you were a back doctor,' the elderly man joked.

'I am—and I'm trained to know when things might not be back problems but other things masquerading as back problems.'

'Think I've got kidney trouble, do you? Had it once—didn't feel like this.'

Hugh took a stethoscope out of his desk drawer and listened to Mr Parkin's chest, and then down his abdomen. Sure enough, there was an audible pulsation away from the midline, and in the right groin there was an area of blue skin over where the blood vessels and nerves left the abdomen and passed down the leg.

Hugh felt a chill of apprehension. Unless he was very much mistaken, Mr Parkin was suffering from a leaking aortic aneurism and unless he was treated very promptly he was extremely likely to die.

Hugh put his hand on Mr Parkin's shoulder and squeezed reassuringly. 'Mr Parkin, I really don't think this is your back, you know.'

'What do you think, then, Mr Barber? Is it a hernia? It definitely happened when I lifted that bag.'

Hugh nodded. 'Yes, I'm sure, but I don't think it's a hernia either. I think a blood vessel in your tum might have sprung a little leak. I may be mistaken, but to be on the safe side you should get it looked at. Now, if you'd just like to stay here for a moment I'll ring your GP and have a little chat to him, OK? I'll be back in a moment.'

He spread a blanket over his patient, went out into the hall and found Judith in the waiting room, straightening magazines and chatting to Dr Knights. 'Judith, have we got Mr Parkin's GP's number on the records?' he asked her softly. 'I think he may have an aortic aneurysm and, if I'm right, it's leaking like a stuck pig.'

Dr Knights leant forwards. 'Excuse me—did I hear you say you'd got a patient with a leaking aneurysm? Want me to have a look?'

Hugh frowned at him thoughtfully. 'You're a doctor,

of course, aren't you? Would you be able to tell just by looking at him?'

He laughed. 'I should hope so. I work in A and E—we see enough of them.'

Hugh sighed with relief. 'Just the man. Would you mind? I'm sorry to do this to you but I'm very concerned about him.'

As they crossed to the consulting room Hugh filled the other man in on the patient's history, and when they went in Hugh introduced him.

'I've hijacked one of the other patients to see you, Mr Parkin. This is Dr Knights. He's kindly agreed to look at you for me to see if he thinks you should see someone before we go to the bother of sending you along to your GP.'

Mr Parkin smiled a little uneasily. 'Fine. Excellent service. Beats waiting in the doctor's surgery. Have you got a dentist out there, Mr Barber? I've been having a bit of toothache.'

They all chuckled, but not for long. Dr Knights turned back the blanket, palpated Mr Parkin's abdomen gently, examined the blue stain in his groin and shook his head. 'I'm sorry, Mr Parkin, I'm afraid Mr Barber's right. You're going to have to go into hospital and get this sorted out today. There's no doubt about it—you've got a leak in there somewhere and it'll need to be mended pretty quickly.'

The man's brows creased. 'It can't be. Surely I'd feel ill?'

'Not necessarily. Not everyone does at this stage.'

'Is it dangerous?' Mr Parkin asked, fear dawning in his eyes.

'Not necessarily—not if the leak was contained by the membrane around the vessel. You might just have a bad backache then, and as long as things continue like that you'll be fine, but you do need to go to hospital.'

'Well, if it gets rid of this killer backache I'll gladly go,' the patient agreed.

Hugh and Dr Knights exchanged glances, and Hugh thought what an appropriate choice of words that was. 'Right—I'll get Judith to call an ambulance. Would you like to ring your wife? Get her to meet you there with some things?'

'You are sure?' he asked again, looking at the doctor.

'Certain,' Dr Knights said emphatically. 'I would love to be proved wrong, but it's showing all the classic symptoms.'

'Better get on with it, then,' Mr Parkin said, and laid his head down again in resignation. 'Yes, ring my wife, Mr Barber. She flaps but she's a good sort. She'll want to be there.'

Hugh went into the hall and sighed, then crossed over to Judith.

'Well?' she asked immediately.

'Dr Knights agrees. Call an ambulance, would you? And his wife—and put it gently. He says she flaps.'

Judith smiled, and Hugh felt some of the weight taken from his shoulders. 'Don't worry, I can handle it,' she said, and reached for the phone.

Hugh, knowing the job was being done and being done well, went back in to his patient and sent up a quick word of thanks that he had some professional help here on the spot—because if that aneurysm should burst in a major way he was going to end up with a death in the surgery unless they were all very lucky.

The ambulance arrived in time, however, and he went on to treat Dr Knights free of charge in exchange for services rendered.

'Do you make any money?' Judith asked teasingly as he let another pensioner out of the door under the illusion that he had been treated under the health service.

He grinned. 'Enough. Talking of money, I owe you your pay.'

'Mmm. I'm going to buy a decent pillow. I'm sure that's why I get headaches.'

Hugh cocked his head on one side and eyed her thoughtfully. 'Want to do me a favour? I've got two different pillows on trial from an orthopaedic bedding firm—would you like to be a guinea pig? Use one the first week and one the second, and see how you get on? Then you can have the one you like—all you have to do is fill in a report form.'

And all I have to do, he thought, is picture you lying on them and I'll go stark, staring mad. . .

CHAPTER SIX

THEY learned on Monday that Mr Parkin had had an operation on Friday afternoon to repair the leak in his aorta and graft a mesh support over the blood vessel, and that as far as one could tell it had been successful. It had also, they gathered, been done in the nick of time.

'Thank God for that,' Hugh said when Judith told him as they sat down to lunch. 'There was a time there when I don't mind admitting I was scared spitless!'

She returned his grin. 'Me too. I don't think I've ever seen a dead person. I wondered if your Mr Parkin was going to be my first.'

'Well, it seems not. Thank goodness he came and saw me and didn't just go to bed with some aspirin.'

'Absolutely—and talking of going to bed, that pillow you gave me is wonderful.'

'Which?'

She flapped her hand dismissively. 'I can't remember. I'll make a note and try the other one, but my neck's been much more comfortable. I've actually enjoyed going to bed.'

He gave a muffled cough of laughter. 'Would you care to rephrase that?' he said, his eyes flickering with something more than humour. She flushed and looked down into her soup. What a thing to say! All she'd been able to think about since Thursday had been going to bed—and not with a pillow! And here he was, grinning at her and making jokes about it.

'You know what I mean,' she mumbled.

'Hey.' His voice was soft, rasping slightly, and his fingers caught her chin and tipped her head up so she had to look at him. 'I'm sorry. I didn't mean to tease you. I'm really glad the pillow helps you sleep.'

Not as much as having you there would, she wanted to say, but bit her tongue. There was a limit to what she wanted him to know about her feelings. She stood up, scraping her chair back on the tiles, took their plates over to the dishwasher and stacked them.

'Tea or coffee?' she asked, trying to change the subject.

'Tea. Look, Judith, about that kiss.'

'It should never have happened,' they both said at once, and then laughed a little self-consciously.

She felt his hands on her shoulders, stilling her restless fidgeting with the teapot.

'I didn't mean to kiss you,' he murmured. 'I certainly didn't mean it to get so out of hand, and there are all sorts of sound and sensible reasons why we shouldn't get involved.'

Her pride was burning bright flags in her cheeks, but she kept her chin up and her back ramrod straight. 'That's all right. You don't have to explain. It was an accident, a one-off, a mistake. It didn't mean anything, I realise that. I do understand, Hugh.'

He was silent for a moment, then very gently but very firmly he turned her round to face him. 'No,' he said softly, 'I don't think you do understand. It wasn't an accident. And it did mean something. It meant a great deal—at least to me.

'It's just the kids—they're all so vulnerable, dependent. They expect the status quo to remain undisturbed, and if we were to allow our relationship to develop it would naturally disturb it. I think we want to be absolutely sure we want that to happen before we make any moves that could rock the boat to that extent. They've all had quite enough to cope with in their lives already.'

'I don't want to rock anybody's boat,' she told him quietly.

His fingers tipped her chin up. 'Judith? Look at me.'

She looked up—into those brilliant blue flames. 'I do,' he said with quiet honesty. 'I want to rock your boat, disturb your status quo, change the even tenor of your life beyond recognition—but I don't think you want that from me, at least not yet.'

She closed her eyes, unable to look at him. 'I don't know what I want from you, Hugh,' she whispered hoarsely.

Just love me, she wanted to cry out. Take me in your arms and love me—make me feel like a woman. Cherish me. . .

His fingertip traced the shape of her eyebrow, then down over her cheek-bone to the corner of her mouth. She felt the tug of his thumb across her lower lip, and without thinking she flicked her tongue out and moistened it.

He gave a muffled groan, and then she heard her name—or felt it in the soft, soundless exhalation of breath across her face. Then his hand fell away, and he stepped back, releasing her. 'Judith, this is crazy,' he muttered, his voice strangled. 'I'm going out for a walk. There are some letters by the computer that need typing up for the post tonight. I'll see you in a bit.'

And he turned on his heel and left her standing there in the empty kitchen, frustrated beyond reason because he had done the sensible thing.

She didn't want to be sensible!

He was going to go nuts. Either that, or he was going to make love to her—one or the other. He pushed the supermarket trolley round, tugging things aimlessly off the shelves. Toothpaste. They needed toothpaste. He turned up the pharmacy aisle and found himself confronted by a rack of condoms.

For what seemed like an age he stared at them and

then, surrendering to the inevitable, he selected a packet and threw them in the trolley. They didn't have to use them, after all—it was just madness not to have some. Just in case things got out of hand. . .

He grabbed a few other things from the frozen food section and went to the checkout, only to discover as he was throwing the purchases on the conveyor belt that the checkout operator was a patient. They chatted for a few seconds, then he watched in horror as the condoms drifted down the conveyor belt straight into her hand.

Bless her, she didn't turn a hair. He did. His neck brick-red, he vowed that if he ever had the need to buy any more he would drive to another town and go to a chemist's shop he never, ever visited. Perhaps that way his private thoughts might remain just that. . .

'You've got a new patient this morning,' Judith told Hugh. He hesitated and came back to her desk—reluctantly, she thought. Oh, dear, was it going to be difficult working with him after their talk on Monday? She had hoped their day apart while he did his children's clinic would give them a breathing space, but things seemed every bit as difficult today as she had imagined they could be. Was he going to avoid her and not look her in the eye and keep a safe distance between them at all times?

Probably. He glanced down at the book, his long, blunt finger tracking down the page until he reached the girl's name. His cuff was turned back and Judith felt an irrational urge to reach out and run her fingertips over the strong, hair-strewn wrist. Madness.

'Naomi Stanton?' he said. 'Any idea what the problem is?'

'Mmm. She broke her arm about ten weeks ago. She was fine at first but it's got worse and worse. She can't touch it now and her mother's worried to death. The hospital X-rays show a perfect mend, and they've said there's nothing they can do. If it still hurts in three months they'll cut the nerve or something.'

'Sounds a bit drastic. How old is she?'

'Thirteen.'

'Hell's teeth. Well, I'll have a look. She might have trapped a nerve in the elbow or something—any complaint of back or neck pain?'

Judith shook her head. 'Not that the mother reported. She's an ex-patient, by the way. Says you treated her successfully three years ago.'

'OK. I'll try and get ahead a little so I can give her longer—who's after her? Oh, George. He's always late. Good. Right.'

He hovered for a second, then with a decisive nod he walked into his office and shut the door with a little click.

Judith let her breath out in a rush. She hadn't even been aware of holding it, but she must have been. Chemistry, she thought, was a very underrated science. It was certainly playing hell with her peace of mind today—or maybe it was something to do with that lean, hairy wrist being shoved under her nose at this time of the morning—

The phone rang, distracting her, and she forced herself to concentrate. At five to eleven, just as Hugh had finished with the previous patient, Mrs Stanton and her daughter came in. The daughter was holding her arm very awkwardly out from her side, and her sweatshirt sleeve was pulled up so that her arm was bare.

It looked, Judith thought, quite normal, and yet it was obviously giving her some pain, if the way she was holding it was anything to go by. She sent them into the waiting room, told Hugh they had arrived and then when all was quiet she disappeared into the kitchen and put the kettle on. Hugh would be busy for a while, but she was gasping for a cup of tea and couldn't see a time when he would be able to stop.

Good. The last thing she needed at the moment was to

sit with him in an uneasy silence and not be able to look him in the eye.

She took her tea back to the office, settled down at the computer and keyed in some of the referral letters and insurance company reports that Hugh had put there on Monday for her to deal with. The phone was mercifully silent, the doorbell didn't ring and she was able to make some significant headway before Hugh emerged from his consulting room.

She looked up as he walked in. He came over and perched on the edge of her desk, folded his arms and grinned, looking disgustingly pleased with himself. 'Well, I found that young lady's problem,' he said smugly.

She sat back and returned the smile. 'Really?'

'Really. She'd got an acute spinal lesion at T4-5 level.'

Judith's brows twitched together. 'Translate, please?'

'She had a problem between her shoulder blades, a locked-up joint between her fourth and fifth thoracic vertebrae. Ten minutes after I unlocked it she said the pain in her arm had gone. In fact, she was so relieved she burst into tears.'

'Poor kid,' Judith said softly. 'She must have been really scared with all that pain for so long. What caused it?'

He shrugged. 'Who knows? The fall that broke it? Wearing a sling? Having a heavy cast hanging on her arm? It could be almost anything. Whatever, she's much better now. She's coming back in a week for a check-up to make sure it's all still moving freely, and I'll give her a thorough going-over then, but in the meantime she's just going to take it easy and enjoy not hurting.'

Judith stood up. 'I'll go and make her next appointment—there's some tea in the pot. It might still be warm enough. George hasn't turned up yet so you've got a minute.'

'Great. Thanks.'

She walked past him just as he stood up, his body tall and lean and very close, and her breath jammed in her chest and she had to remind her legs how to walk because they didn't seem to want to leave the room.

Idiot woman, she scolded herself. He's just a man. He's your boss. Get yourself under control!

Hugh went into the kitchen, braced his hands on the edge of the worktop and let his head hang. How could he want her so much? It was crazy. When she'd stood up and squeezed past him, and he'd got to his feet to move out of her way, he'd been just millimetres from that soft, yielding body that he ached to lose himself in. He'd hardly been able to breathe, never mind walk and talk.

Idiot man, he scolded himself. She's just a woman. She's your employee. Get yourself under control!

Judith made their lunch and wondered if she'd get away with taking hers out into the garden and pleading a headache and the need for fresh air.

Probably not. If she told him she had a headache he'd want to look at her neck again, and the very thought of his hands touching her was enough to send her reason screaming off into the middle distance. No. She'd sit there on the other side of the table and behave herself.

She would. Definitely. Absolutely. Yes.

No. Hugh came in, slouched into the chair with a big sigh and grinned at her tiredly—and her resolve turned to mush.

'Bad morning?' she asked, itching to reach out and touch his hand where it lay on the edge of the table.

He laughed softly, without humour. 'No, not really. One or two miracle cures, one or two back to square one because they won't take advice—the same old story. No, I guess I'm just tired. I haven't been sleeping very well.'

Their eyes clashed, heat flaring between them. 'Neither have I,' she confessed.

'Oh, hell, Judith,' he murmured, and then somehow he was on his feet on her side of the table, pulling her up against him and into his arms. Their mouths met and locked and there was no hesitation, no pussyfooting around, no careful reserve. Just two people with the same need, the same desperate longing to be one.

The result was a foregone conclusion. Afterwards Judith wondered how they'd lasted that long but just then she couldn't think, couldn't speak, could hardly breathe.

With a muffled oath Hugh swung her up into his arms, ran up the stairs and shouldered open a door, then kicked it shut behind them. She noticed inconsequentially that the walls were a soft terracotta colour, and then her surroundings disappeared and she was aware only of the soft quilt beneath her back and Hugh's welcome weight pressing her into the mattress.

His mouth found hers again, clamouring for more, and she gave him all she had, all she was, all she could be. Their hands plucked feverishly at clothes until with a ragged curse Hugh knelt up, pulled her to a sitting position and undressed her with desperate haste. His own clothes were flung away, discarded without thought, and then their lips met again, their bodies aligned with a sigh of relief and then, curiously, he was still.

'Lord, you feel so good, Judith,' he whispered unevenly. His hands stroked gently over her body, lingering here and there—exploring her with exquisite sensitivity.

It drove her crazy. It was far worse than the haste, far more potent than the urgency had been. This fire burned deeper, slower, hotter than the one before—than any fire had ever burned.

She reached for him, running her palms curiously over the hot, velvety skin that cloaked his virile frame. She could feel the muscles bunching, the taut sinews, the thunder of his heart shaking his whole body—and she could feel her own heart, thrashing out of control, desperate for something—

'Hugh?' she whispered. 'Hugh, please. . .'

He moved over her, his body trembling beneath her hands, and then they were gloriously one—moving together towards that elusive goal.

She reached it seconds before him, falling headlong into a shattering release that drove him over the edge. He shuddered convulsively, then a deep, guttural cry was torn from his chest and he fell against her, his head dropping into the crook of her shoulder.

'Too heavy,' he muttered, and then his arms tightened around her, cradling her to him as he rolled to his side and collapsed against the pillows.

Gradually their breathing slowed, their hearts steadied and their trembling ceased. Then Judith felt his hand brush her cheek and her eyes flickered open. His face was inches from hers, his eyes burning brightly as they locked with her clear grey gaze.

'OK?' he murmured.

OK? She'd never be the same again, but OK? Probably. She nodded. 'You?'

His smile was worth waiting for. 'Never better. I mean that, Judith. I've never felt like this in my life.'

She swallowed. 'Not even with your wife?' she asked quietly.

He was silent for a moment. 'Maybe with Linda. I don't know. I can't remember. I don't think so.'

She reached out and caressed his face, unbelievably touched by his admission. 'I haven't, I know that. It's never been like that. There was only ever Mike, and we were just kids. We didn't know where to begin.'

His lips brushed hers, lightly, like thistledown. 'I thought I'd go crazy for you,' he admitted gruffly.

'I couldn't think about anything else.'

'Nor could I.'

They shared a smile and he kissed her again, more deeply this time, then settled her head against his chest. She could feel the steady beating of his heart, a slow, normal rhythm now—unlike the earlier dance of madness.

'I want you again,' he murmured.

Reason struggled to the surface. 'Hugh, there isn't time. The patients. . .'

He swore, softly and without real heat. Then he hugged her briefly and eased away, swinging his legs over the side of the bed and running his hands through his hair. Then he looked around the room and chuckled. 'Were we in a hurry or what?' he said, staring at the scattered clothes with an expression of amused disbelief.

Judith lifted herself up onto one elbow and looked around. 'Mmm,' she agreed with a satisfied grin. 'I'd say we were in a hurry.'

They laughed, an intimate, cosy sound that made her feel warm inside. Then he leant over and kissed her, and his hand patted her bare bottom lightly. 'Up you get, sweets. If you like there stretched out like that, looking edible, we won't get downstairs before tomorrow morning.'

Edible? A humourless little laugh escaped her. 'Hugh, I'm fat,' she told him bluntly.

His eyes raked her body, his response immediate and flattering. 'Codswallop,' he said without hesitation. 'You're beautiful. Soft and full and all woman. For God's sake, get yourself covered up while I'll still let you.'

She bounced out of the bed, feeling gloriously alive and free, truly happy with herself for the first time in ages—years, probably. Maybe even longer. Humming softly, she pulled on her clothes, and marvelled that her tights weren't shredded beyond redemption and her blouse had only lost one button and that below the waist.

Then Hugh tugged the bed straight, winked at her and held out his hand. 'Come on, temptress, let's get you out of this den of iniquity before I'm led astray again—much as I want to be.'

'There's always tomorrow,' she said brazenly, and he laughed, a raw and rather breathless sound.

'And don't I know it.' He hesitated at the doorway. 'Look—we've been a little rash here today,' he murmured. 'I bought some condoms the other day in the supermarket but I forgot all about them. If anything happens. . .'

'It won't,' she assured him confidently. 'Don't worry. It's safe at the moment.'

'Truly?'

'Truly. Hugh, don't worry. I wouldn't lie to you.'

'No.' He pulled her into his arms and hugged her gently, then turned her towards the door, steering her down the stairs and into the kitchen. 'Put the kettle on and then go and brush your hair and straighten your face. You look as if you've just been rumpled in a haystack.'

'Well, there's a surprise,' she said, answering his grin with one of her own. 'You look pretty rumpled yourself.'

She plugged in the kettle and went into the cloakroom and stared despairingly at her reflection. The hair and lips she could fix. She could even disguise the faint trace of whisker burn on her chin, but what could she do about the light in her eyes?

She looked, she thought—assessing herself frankly—like a woman in love, and there was no way she was going to be able to disguise that. She sorted out her hair, put on a streak of soft rose lipstick, dabbed a touch of foundation over the whisker-burn and went back to the office.

Hugh looked up, forgot what he was saying and told the person on the other end of the phone that something had just come up and he'd call back. Then he cradled the receiver, slouched back in the chair and threw her a sexy grin. Lord, he looked gorgeous—

'Something's come up, eh?' she teased.

'Mmm. Surprise, surprise.'

She blushed a little, secretly delighted at his reaction. 'Having trouble concentrating?' she asked him.

'Too right. I keep losing the thread—not that that's any surprise. You look so beautiful you're enough to distract a robot.'

She chuckled. 'You're biased. I don't look beautiful at all. I look—well, rumpled, as you said.'

He stood up, came round the desk and pulled her gently into his arms. 'You look as if you've been soundly loved. It suits you.'

She held her hand over his mouth. 'Uh-uh. Don't kiss me. I've repaired the damage once already.'

'Rationed now, am I?'

She laughed. 'Yes. Anyway, you've got a phone call to finish. I'll go in the kitchen and make us some lunch.'

He shook his head. 'There isn't time. Forget about lunch. Just cook extra for this evening. I want to have a look at Woody tonight as well. Perhaps I'll do that after we eat.'

'OK. Shall I make coffee?'

He grinned and swooped down, dropping a kiss on her unsuspecting lips before he let her go. 'Good idea. I'll make that call. And, Judith?'

She quirked a brow.

'Don't come back in until I'm off the phone. I can't mess the call up twice running.'

She grinned, turned on her heel and wiggled out of the door, enjoying her power. A muffled groan of laughter was her reward, then the door clicked firmly shut behind her.

*   *   *

'OK. Woody, how've you been?'

Woody, sitting on the edge of the treatment table, lifted a shoulder fractionally. 'Better, I think. Not just my back, but I seem to be able to walk better, and sometimes— nah, it's silly.'

'What?'

The boy shook his head, but Hugh persisted. 'What?' he asked again.

'Sometimes I think I can talk better—quicker, you know? My jaw feels more co-operative, and I can swallow better.'

Hugh nodded. 'Good. That's quite possible. I've done quite a lot of work into your neck and face muscles, so it would seem reasonable, and your cranium's moving more freely, too. How are the psoas muscles?'

Woody's grin was crooked and endearing. 'Still tight.'

'OK. Lie down on your side and let's have a look at things.'

Yes, he thought, working through the muscle groups and checking the movement in each joint in turn, there did seem to be a steady and sustained improvement. He freed the iliopsoas muscles that ran down the abdomen from inside the hip-bone and kept tightening and tipping Woody forwards, then worked on his face and neck for a while. Eventually seating himself at the end, he took Woody's head lightly in his hands and worked on his cranial rhythm for a while.

Oh, yes, it was better, he thought in satisfaction. Much better.

He freed a blocked sinus, got the system flowing well again and then sat him up. 'OK?'

Woody grinned and nodded. 'Yeah. That's so relaxing.'

'It's meant to be. Some of my Tuesday children fall asleep. Mind you, a lot of them are very young—some are babies.'

'Aren't you scared, treating babies?'

Hugh smiled at him. 'Scared? No. I love babies. They have very sensitive, responsive systems. They're very rewarding to treat.'

Woody looked thoughtful for a moment, then said, 'If you'd treated me when I was a baby would I have been all right?'

Hugh sat beside him on the edge of the couch and put a hand on his shoulder. 'No. I don't think it would have made a significant difference. Your problems arose, I think, because your mother had a long and difficult labour. I might have been able to help you with mobility, but I couldn't have reversed any neurological damage, Edward.'

Woody nodded. 'I thought not. I just wanted to know for sure.' He looked at Hugh. 'Mum blames herself.'

'I know.'

'It wasn't her fault. They should have helped her.'

Hugh looked down at his hands and found they were clenched. He made them relax. 'Yes, they should. Are you bitter about it?'

He shrugged. 'Sometimes. They were all kids. Kids don't think, do they? They just act and react. I'm used to that.'

His words sounded as if they were lifted straight from a psychologist's manual, Hugh thought. He'd probably been told things like that in connection with his treatment by others over and over again in his short life.

Damn. He was such a nice kid.

'How about a game of chess?' Hugh offered.

Woody looked at him searchingly. 'Do you play?'

He nodded. 'Sometimes.'

'OK.'

Hugh went back to the kitchen and took the chess set out of the kitchen drawer. Toots was helping Judith make an apple pie, and there was no sign of Martin. Hopefully he was doing his homework without having to have World

War III first. While there's life, Hugh thought.

Woody came in, they sat down and Hugh focussed on the pieces. There was no way he was going to underestimate this lad!

Judith put the pie in the oven, bathed Alice and put her to bed with a long story. She came back to the kitchen to find Hugh and Woody still bent over the table, with Martin sitting at one end watching their moves. She made them tea, sat down at the other end of the table and watched them all.

Martin's face, particularly, spoke volumes. Oh, dear, she thought, he's jealous. Jealous of Woody because he's taken his place, jealous of Woody's ability at chess because he was about to beat Hugh and they all knew it, and jealous of the attention that was being focussed on the players and not him.

He looked up and Judith caught his eye and winked. He didn't return her smile. Instead he looked away, just as Woody leant across, placed a piece and said, 'Checkmate,' with quiet satisfaction.

Hugh's brows creased for a second, then he gave a little grunt and sat back. 'Well done. I didn't see that coming at all.'

Woody grinned and set the pieces up again. 'Want to redeem your honour?'

'Hugh, we ought to go,' she said, catching sight of Martin's face. 'Play with Martin if you want another game.'

'Nah—I've got homework,' Martin said dismissively. 'Actually, Dad, I could do with a hand. It's my IT.'

'Computers?' Hugh frowned doubtfully. 'I don't know if I can help—what are you stuck on?'

'There's a question about graphics—I don't understand it.'

'Want me to give you a hand?' Woody offered.

Judith held her breath. Martin looked at Woody as if

he were an alien, then shrugged. 'Will you know where to start?'

'I should think so. Where's your computer?'

'In my bedroom—upstairs, in the attic.'

'Come on, then.'

Martin looked at him in amazement. 'Can you get upstairs?'

Woody sighed. 'Of course I can. It just takes longer— like everything else.'

'Didn't take you long to thrash Dad at chess,' Martin said resentfully.

Woody laughed, a high-pitched, cracked laugh that made Martin wince. 'He wasn't concentrating. I think he's tired or something.'

They left the room and Hugh met Judith's eye. 'Definitely "or something". I was doing fine till you came back in and I could see your cleavage out of the corner of my eye,' he said softly.

She chuckled, then thought of Martin's reaction and sobered. 'Hugh, Martin's jealous.'

'I know.'

'Play chess with him when we've gone.'

'And let him beat me?'

She looked him in the eye. 'If that's what it takes.'

'I can't. He always knows.'

'So beat him, but only just, or get into stalemate.'

He nodded. 'Yes. You're right. God, teenagers are so convoluted. Do you suppose they're all right up there?'

'I expect so. Edward's good with computers. It's our one extravagance, and it's been a godsend. It's given him so much confidence.'

'Does he play chess with it?' Hugh asked mildly.

Judith laughed. 'Endlessly. It's improved his skill no end. Want to borrow the CD to download it onto your computer?'

Hugh chuckled. 'No. He'll spend hours practising

and then he'll thrash me. My ego's too frail.'

'Oh, poor baby.'

'Which reminds me, where's Toots?'

'In bed.' She drew a circle on the table with a drip of tea, wondering how to broach the next topic and deciding in the end just to ask. 'Hugh?' she said softly.

'Mmm?'

'Tell me about how Linda died.'

He went still for a moment, then pushed back his chair, held out his hand to her and led her over to the little sofa.

They sat down side by side and he kept her hand in his, wrapped against his thigh. 'She had a bad heart,' he said quietly. 'We found out after she had Martin that she had a murmur, and she was told never to have any more children because of the strain on her heart. They think she might have had bacterial endocarditis when she was younger, which they'd thought was flu.

'Anyway, six years passed and she grew more and more withdrawn. Then one weekend we were away with friends and she got me a little bit drunk and seduced me. I forgot all about birth control, of course—I seem to make a habit of that—and afterwards she confessed she'd done it on purpose to get pregnant.'

'And was she?'

'Yes—with Toots. Anyway her heart deteriorated suddenly towards the end of her pregnancy, they took her into hospital and she ended up in intensive care. She was on oxygen and they were just considering doing a Caesarean section with an epidural when she arrested.'

'Oh, dear God, Hugh. Whatever did they do?'

'There was nothing they could do. They put her on a ventilator, kept her heart going manually and delivered Toots on the spot. As soon as she was born they let Linda go.'

Judith closed her eyes, the bright unshed tears spilling over her cheeks and splashing into her lap. 'Oh, Hugh,

I'm so sorry. Whatever did you do?'

He sighed raggedly. 'I took my baby home to Martin and we got on with our lives. Bit by bit, inch by inch, day by day—you know how it is.'

She did know how it was, but, even so, to cope alone with that weight of grief—

'Did you have anyone to help you?'

'Oh, yes. My parents and Linda's parents have been marvellous. They took it in turns to look after her, one or other mum coming to stay for a week at a time until I was back on my feet and we'd got a nanny organised. Now Toots is at school it's easier, but the holidays are still difficult and I do feel guilty about the amount of time they're on their own at the end of the day.

'Christine used to have to shoot off at four to get her other two kids, you see, so when you turned up and were available it really was a godsend. Anyway, they're more independent now but Martin, more than Toots, really suffered from losing his mother. Poor old Toots, of course, has never known what it is to have a mother.'

'Like Woody's never had a father. It is tough, but I'm sure the love and warmth of one good parent is worth far more than the indifference of two bad ones.'

His arm slipped round her shoulders and he hugged her gently. 'I'm sure you're right. We just do what we have to do. It's just that there are times when being a good parent isn't easy, and it would be so much easier with someone to share the burden—and the joys.'

Judith swallowed. Oh, yes, she thought, how good it would be to have someone to share it all with.

Someone like Hugh. . .

CHAPTER SEVEN

'GOODBYE, Mr Turner. See you next week.'

The outer front door closed behind the patient with a decisive click, and Hugh turned to Judith. The message in his eyes was unmistakable, and her mouth felt suddenly dry with tension.

'Come to bed with me,' he said softly.

'Hugh, this is crazy,' she began, but he cut her off.

'No. It's not crazy. It's our time, just for us. God knows neither of us has much of that.' He held out his hand towards her, palm up, and she stood up and walked over to him. He was right. This was their time, and they'd earned it.

She put her hand in his, and felt the leap of her heart as his fingers closed round hers and squeezed comfortingly. He led her to his room, undressed her slowly and carefully and then drew her into his arms.

'You feel so good,' he murmured, his hands skimming down her spine to settle over her hips—easing her closer. His lips drifted over her skin, caressing her jaw, her neck, the hollow of her throat. . .

'Don't you feel just a little overdressed?' she said breathlessly, pushing him gently away.

He chuckled. 'Just a bit.' His clothes were dispatched without ceremony, and then he drew her into his arms again. 'That's better,' he murmured. 'I can really feel you now.'

Judith was just thinking the same thing, revelling in the differences between them. His limbs were hard where hers were soft, his skin was hotter and dusted with coarse, wiry hair where hers was baby-smooth. His body was lean and flat, his ribcage deep, where her body curved and flowed.

Like night and day, yin and yang, they completed and complemented each other, and suddenly she was proud of her softness, her womanly curves and lush fullness. Hugh, certainly, seemed to find them fascinating, lavishing attention on her body with gentle, slow hands that cherished every inch of her sensitive and craving skin.

He explored her thoroughly, worshipped her almost, and as the last echoes of their passion died away she felt more complete than she had ever felt in her life.

He held her tenderly against his chest, his hands still moving slowly over her body—soothing her now and guiding her carefully back down to earth. 'OK?' he murmured.

'Mmm. Wonderful. It was even better than before.'

'I know.'

They fell silent then, content just to hold each other in the few minutes left before they had to put on the trappings of reality and face the world again. It was like a dream, a stolen moment when they could be themselves instead of the people they had had to become.

It was so rare, so precious, so fleeting that Judith wanted to cry. Instead she wrapped the memory deep in her heart and saved it for the time to come when she would be alone again—when Hugh had moved on and all this was nothing more than a distant memory.

It became a pattern. On Mondays and Thursdays, if the radiographer had gone, and on Wednesdays and Fridays come what may, Hugh would close the outer door, hold out his hand and lead Judith to paradise. They started switching on the answering machine to make sure not even the phone disturbed them, and they would lie in Hugh's big bed and make love lazily and talk about nothing and everything.

And gradually, with every day that passed, Judith grew to love Hugh more and more.

She loved his children, too. Alice was easy to love, dear little thing that she was, with her guileless blue eyes and innocent face hiding abundant mischief. Judith adored her, the little pixie, and she in turn began to shadow Woody whenever he was there. She sat next to him and showed him whatever gawdy confection she had made at school in art, and he gave her his undivided attention and became every bit as smitten.

Only Martin maintained a distance, and as time went on Judith became more and more concerned about it. Half-term was coming up and Hugh was closing the surgery for the last few days so he would have a long weekend with the children.

'We're going to Wales to a friend's cottage—why don't you come?' he suggested.

She was tempted. Oh, how she was tempted, but she felt Martin needed time alone with his father without Woody stealing his thunder and getting on his nerves, as he undoubtedly did. And anyway, it was Woody's birthday and she wanted them to be together. 'I don't think so. Not this time,' she said, her voice gentle to soften the blow.

'Kids again,' Hugh said flatly. 'Oh, hell, Judith, I just want to spend some time with you. Not just a stolen half-hour but real time—days—nights.'

She looked into those burning blue eyes and could have wept. 'Woody's got a friend—Al. He stays with him sometimes.'

Hugh nodded slowly. 'The kids could go to my parents for a weekend. They keep asking. In fact, Marty's got a weekend coming up with a rugby tour soon. Maybe they could have Toots if Al's parents could have Woody at the same time.'

'I'll ask Belle. When is it?'

'Second weekend in November—Friday and Satuday nights.'

'OK.'

'We could go away,' he said softly. 'Book a hotel and go and be pampered. No cooking, no washing-up—nothing to think about but whether or not we're going to get up.'

It sounded so wonderful she could almost taste it. 'Don't,' she groaned theatrically.

'Tempted?'

She laughed. 'Just a bit.'

He pulled her into his arms and hugged her. 'We'll fix it, sweetheart. We'll have some time, don't worry. Just hang on in there.'

So she did. He went to Wales with his children, and Woody played with his new computer game, and she missed Hugh unbearably.

So, apparently, did his patients. The phone never stopped ringing from the moment they were back at work, and to fit everybody in he worked until seven for the whole of the following week.

That, of course, had its upside and downside. For Toots it was wonderful because she got to spend time with Woody, and for Hugh and Judith, of course, it meant extra time together for the few moments between patients when he was out of the consulting room.

For Woody and Martin, though, it meant they were thrust into each other's company, and they both found that hard. They did try to work things out but Woody consistently beat Martin at chess, despite the game installed on Martin's computer so he could practise, and Martin took great delight in charging upstairs three at a time and leaving Woody trailing far behind.

Judith, from her desk at the bottom of the stairs near the snug door, watched all this byplay and worried for them both. They were like chalk and cheese—Woody, who would have been quietly intellectual and more intro-spective regardless of his disability, and Martin, physical and immediate, who rushed from one thing to another without thought or reason, grabbing life by the throat and impatient with anything that required careful deliberation.

He was clever, Judith realised, but lacked Woody's quiet perseverance. His father was the same with every-thing except his patients. With them, though, he found the patience to persist until he had broken through and made a difference.

Some patients, of course, were easily cured, like Naomi Stanton with her hypersensitive arm which he had relieved with one treatment. Others, like the upholsterer who continually handled heavy furniture and rolls of fabric and often worked at awkward angles, were harder to help and impossible to cure.

And then there was Mr Parkin, who came in one day to see them, looking remarkably chipper and bearing a bottle of champagne. 'I would have brought you a case but I didn't dare lift it,' he told Hugh with a laugh. 'Anyway, I just wanted to thank you for saving my life—you did, you know. Did you realise how close I got?'

Hugh gave a wry smile and nodded. 'Oh, yes, I knew. You gave me a nasty turn there, Mr Parkin.'

'You and me both, skipper,' the man said with a smile. 'Still, I'm all right now and the wife's finally stopped flapping so we can start getting back to normal.'

'Good. And thank you for the champagne.'

'My pleasure. It's a nice one—save it for a special moment.'

Hugh chuckled. 'I will.'

They watched him leave, then turned to smile at each other. 'He's looking good.'

'Yes.' Hugh hefted the bottle of champagne. 'So's this. I'll put it in the utility room. He's right, it is a nice one. We'll have to find the psychological moment.'

Their eyes clashed, and Judith's mind conjured a shamelessly romantic and sensuous scene. Soft colour brushed her cheeks, and Hugh's laugh was husky and intimate. 'Down, girl,' he murmured. 'There are patients in the waiting room. Behave.'

'Yessir,' she said cheekily, and reached for the ever-ringing phone. 'Mr Barber's surgery—hello, Christine! How are you? Yes, sure.'

She looked up at Hugh and held the receiver out to him. 'It's Christine.'

He took the phone and handed her the bottle. 'Hi, there. How's tricks? Oh. Is he? Bring him in—no, no, now will do. Anytime. No, of course I can fit you in. Don't worry about it. I'll see you later.'

Judith, headed for the utility room with the champagne, wondered how on earth Hugh imagined he was going to fit in another patient. The book was already hectic, with one fitted in and another on traction. Still, it was up to him. If he felt it was important he would do his best.

He found her in the kitchen. 'Christine's baby's got colic. He's been bad for a week and the health visitor just says he'll grow out of it and she's to stop eating things which upset him, or alternatively wean him. The trouble is she's being very careful with her diet and she doesn't want to wean him.'

'So what can you do?'

'Treat him cranially. It's often remarkable how well it works.'

'Have you got time?'

He shrugged. 'I'll have to make time. I'll do it in the snug with him on my lap. Then if he drops off to sleep he can stay there on the sofa for a while and I can get on.'

They heard the baby arriving a few minutes later, his grizzling cry clear evidence of his misery.

'Come and have a cup of tea until Hugh's ready for you,' Judith said, leading her predecessor into the kitchen.

Christine perched on the sofa and looked at it in amusement. 'So it's still here, then, after I tried to ruin it by having Tim all over it?'

Judith chuckled. 'Oh, yes, it's fine. Martin was a bit shocked, but he's got over it now. Will you still be here when the children get home from school?'

'I doubt it—unless I ring my mum and ask her to pick the others up for me. I'd love to see them again.'

'I know Toots would love to see you, too, and the baby. She was so worried you'd died.'

Christine smoothed her baby's hair back from his face. 'I know. Hugh told me. It's because of her mother, of course. She just thinks childbirth is dangerous. Perhaps I will hang on and see them—to reassure her—unless Tim makes such an ungodly row that we get flung out, of course.'

Tim, right on queue, started to cry again.

Judith put a cup of tea in Christine's hand, took the baby from her, and walked him up and down which seemed to settle him a little. 'Is he hungry?'

She laughed. 'He's probably suffering from being over-fed,' she told Judith. 'Every time he cries I feed him, but he's probably only crying because he's got tummy ache. I just feel it comforts him but, really, I'm at my wits end. Neither of the others were like this.'

'Do you suppose it's because he was early?' Judith asked, pausing in her floor-walking to sip her tea.

'Who knows? All I can tell you is it's a pain. The other two hate him, my husband's threatening to leave home and I'm ready to drop him head down into a bucket.'

'Oh. That good, eh?'

Judith swapped grins with Christine, moving on again as the grizzling started up once more. Then Hugh popped his head round the door and beckoned.

'Right, I've got a little gap—let's make the most of it. Come in the snug, all of you.'

They followed him and found him sitting on the settee with his legs stretched out. 'Right, let's have him.'

Judith handed over the baby and then, hovering between the snug and her post at her desk, watched with interest to see what he would do. She had never seen anyone treated with cranial osteopathy and was fascinated.

Hugh laid the crying baby on the cushions between his legs so that he could reach it easily, and then he cupped the tiny head in his fingers and closed his eyes. After a moment in which Judith thought Hugh wasn't doing anything, the baby's wretched grizzling seemed to quieten a little. Within a few moments he started to relax, his little limbs becoming quite loose and floppy as the tension drained out of him. His crying hiccupped to a halt and then miraculously ceased.

'Oh, yes, little one, that was tight, wasn't it?' Hugh crooned softly.

Judith watched, fascinated, as his fingers moved almost imperceptibly in a slight rippling rhythm, repeating the motion every few seconds. The baby was now completely relaxed, his eyelids drooping, and within minutes he was peacefully asleep. Still Hugh kept working, though, ignoring the time and the queue of patients, until finally he eased his hands away and opened his eyes.

'That's more like it. He was all over the place—I suspect because the birth was so fast his skull bones hadn't moulded evenly and so it had locked up here and there. I'll probably need to see him several times to keep it free until it all settles down—let's just make him comfy and find some time in the book.'

He levered himself up, taking care not to jostle the sleeping baby, then placed a cushion so he couldn't roll off and covered him with the little rug. 'Right, let's look at the appointment book.'

Judith glanced at her watch. 'Why don't Christine and

I find her some slots while you get on with your next
patient? You're running half an hour behind now.'

He looked amazed. 'Did it take that long?'

She smiled and nodded. 'Yes. Come on, I'll make you
a cup of tea and bring it out to the office in a minute.
Mrs Brown's just gone in to wait for you.'

'Thanks—and don't forget, no charge.' He winked at
her and went into his consulting room, leaving them to
sort out appointments.

'Lovely—thank you,' the other woman said as Judith
handed over the card. 'So, how's it going? Hugh told me
you'd stepped into my shoes without warning—he was
so grateful.'

Judith chuckled. 'He was grateful? I needed a job drastically badly. I couldn't believe my luck.' She fiddled
with a pen for a moment, then looked at Christine. 'So,
do you think you'll be coming back to work eventually?'

Christine chewed her lip. 'I don't know. It's so much
more work with three—I don't really know if I could
cope with it—and Hugh's getting busier as well. He's
working longer hours and he needs someone here later—
but you've got a child, haven't you? How are you
managing?'

So Judith told her about their domestic arrangements
for after school, and Christine was impressed. 'Sounds
like you've got it all worked out. I don't suppose you
want to take it on permanently?'

There was nothing Judith wanted more, but not in quite
the way Christine was implying. She made a noncommit-
tal response, sent the other woman to put the kettle on
and left Christine making a cup of tea for herself and
Hugh while she got back to the desk and soothed the
patients who had been held up.

Gradually he worked his way back to time, and then
the children were home and delighted to see Christine and
the baby, who was sleeping peacefully and—according to

Hugh—would probably continue to do so for ages.

'What's his name?' Alice asked.

'Tim.'

'Oh. Hello, Tim.' She prodded him gently but he carried on sleeping, to everyone's relief. Then she turned her huge blue eyes on Christine and produced her pleading look. 'Can I hold him?'

Christine almost melted. 'Well—maybe later if he wakes up. It's just that he's been a little bit poorly and I don't want him to be disturbed now he's sleeping.'

Hugh, arriving at the desk as this was going on, looked into the snug and winked at Christine. 'How's it going?'

'He's really sleeping peacefully—he looks like a different baby.'

'You should have come straight away.'

She smiled. 'I know. I'm sorry.'

'I want to hold him, Daddy,' Alice said, tugging at his sleeve. 'If you wake him up I can hold him—Christine said so.'

He laughed and rumpled her hair. 'I don't think she meant me to wake Tim up just so you can cuddle him, Toots.'

'Oh.' Her little face fell, but Hugh was made of sterner stuff and so was Christine.

'I tell you what, why don't I read you a story and we'll wait for him to wake—OK?' Christine suggested.

So they snuggled up together on a big chair, and through the slightly open door Judith could hear the two of them chatting about the book. It was a very homely little scene and reminded Judith of Woody's childhood—and her own, before her mother had become too busy to read to her.

How long ago that seemed, and how much had changed since she had been that innocent little girl. . .

*   *   *

'Are we going to the fireworks tomorrow?' Martin asked as they at their supper on the Friday evening.

Heavens, Judith thought, was it really that time of year already?

'We usually do,' Hugh said noncommittally. 'Do you want to?'

'Oh, wow, Daddy, excellent!' Alice squeaked, bouncing up and down on her chair.

Judith caught the glass just before it tipped over and suppressed her smile. 'I think that was a yes,' she murmured.

Hugh chuckled. 'I think so, too. Are you going?'

'I don't know. It's up to Edward. Sometimes we do, sometimes we don't.'

Hugh glanced at her son. 'Woody? Want to join us?'

'Oh, yes, Woody, please! Please come!' Alice begged.

Woody glanced from Hugh to his mother, to Alice, to Martin and back to Judith. 'It's up to Mum,' he said.

She tried to read his eyes. 'Can we let you know in the morning?' she suggested.

'Sure. We could pick you up on the way. We usually park as near as we can but then we have to walk the last few hundred yards—we could take your chair, though, Woody, if you didn't want to walk that far.'

Woody shrugged, clearly uncomfortable with the subject.

'I'll ring you,' Judith promised. After she'd talked to her son.

Hugh ran them home, as he was in the habit of doing, and as she got out of the car he caught her hand and held it for a moment. 'Do come,' he murmured. 'See how Woody feels, but it would be good to have you with us. Alice wants him there, and I have to confess I'd love to have you with me.'

She gave a hesitant smile. 'I'll see. I'll talk to you tomorrow. Sleep well.'

'And you.' His thumb caressed the back of her hand briefly and then he let her go. She got out of the car, shut the door and waved him off, then turned back up the path to find Woody disconsolately kicking a stone up the paving to the front door.

She opened the door, waited while he came slowly inside and parked his sticks, then met his eyes. 'Why don't you want to go, darling?' she asked.

He shrugged. 'I think we'd be in the way.'

'In Martin's way.'

He shrugged again.

'Do you often feel that? As if you're in Martin's way?'

'He hates it when his dad talks to me.'

Or plays chess, or treats his back, or any of the other things that took Hugh's time away from Martin. He even seemed to resent the time Alice spent with Woody, Judith thought. Was he really so insecure?

'Would you rather we went alone?'

Woody shook his head. 'It doesn't make sense. You want to be with Hugh.'

Judith, shaken by his observation, went into the kitchen and plugged in the kettle, busying her hands while she thought of something to say.

'Mum, it's all right. You're entitled to a life of your own. I like him. He could be a lot worse.'

She swallowed her nerves. 'So how would you feel about us?' she asked him. 'You know, if we got involved in a relationship?'

'Fine. He's a nice person. He'd be kind to you.'

And how. She looked down at her hands, knotted together on the edge of the worktop, the knuckles white. 'He's asked me to go away with him next weekend. Martin's on a rugby tour with the school, Toots can go to her grandparents and I wondered if you'd like to stay with Al.'

'Sure. Tell me it's none of my business, if you like, but are you having an affair?'

Her knuckles went even whiter. 'You're right, it isn't—but, yes, we are.'

'Good. It's time someone spoiled you a bit. You've been on your own much too long.'

His response stunned her. That was it? No jealousy, no condemnation, no temper tantrums?

She turned to face him, and pulled him into a big hug. 'I love you, Edward.'

'Oh, Mother, not sloppy stuff,' he protested, and she laughed and let him go.

'Sorry. So, about these fireworks tomorrow. . .'

'Can I go to bed and think about it and tell you in the morning?'

She nodded. 'Sure. We need to do your physio first.'

He sighed softly but went to his room and changed into his tracksuit, then came back. They went through the pattern of resisted thrusts and stretches and mobilising exercises, while he bit his lip and forced himself to relax and not fight it.

'I think you're better, you know. You don't seem to have nearly so much tension in some of these muscles. The spasticity's much less marked.'

'That's what Hugh said. He's been doing that cranial stuff—it feels brilliant when he does it, and I feel much better for days afterwards.'

'How, "better"?'

He shrugged. 'More relaxed? Just less worried, more confident, more comfortable. My body works better for me and that makes me feel better.'

'It certainly seems improved,' she agreed, amazed at the difference. It had never occurred to her that Hugh's treatment could help Woody's CP this much. She'd only considered it for the spinal problem and the resulting muscle guarding, not the root cause of his problems. She

sat back on her heels and folded her arms. 'Right, you
can go and get ready for bed now and come back and
watch television with me for a while, if you like.'

'What's on?'

She shrugged. 'Don't know. That forensic science
thing. Why?'

He lifted a shoulder in unconscious imitation of her
gesture. 'I might do something on my computer. There's
a programme I'm trying to run that's giving me trouble.'

'OK,' Judith said with a smile, trying to disguise her
disappointment. She hardly saw anything of him on his
own since she had started working for Hugh. Funny, that.
She'd almost ended up being jealous of herself. How silly!

She rang Hugh next morning, after Woody had
delivered his verdict, and told him that they would be
coming.

'Great,' Hugh said enthusiastically. 'I'm really glad.
We can hold hands in the dark and no one will notice.'

She laughed softly, looking towards Edward's bedroom
door. 'I wouldn't be too sure,' she murmured. 'He guessed
we're having an affair.'

Hugh swore under his breath. 'How? What did he say?'

'He approves of you. Says you'll look after me. Says
it's time someone spoiled me a bit.'

Hugh chuckled in relief. 'Good. For a moment I
thought I was going to be challenged to a duel in defence
of your honour.'

Her smile faded. 'I keep telling you, I don't have any
honour.'

'Rubbish. I'll pick you both up at six-thirty. Don't
forget to wrap up warmly—it's always cold in the park.'

Woody was excited. He loved the fireworks—not the
crowds, the drama and the atmosphere, but the effects—
the spectacular colours, the amazing variety of bangs and
whooshes and fizzes that chemistry could create. He

thought it was possible that he'd want to be a chemist when he grew up. It fascinated him, but people found that hard to understand.

Even Al, whom he loved to death, found his preoccupation with chemistry a bit odd. Oh, well. So he was a bit odd. He'd always known and accepted that.

He pulled his scarf tight round his neck and tucked it into his coat, then looked out of the window. 'They're here,' he called to his mother, and waved at Martin in the back seat of the car. Martin looked at him for a moment, then turned pointedly away.

Rejection, Woody thought, was something one never really got used to.

Slowly, because he did everything slowly, he unzipped his coat and pulled his scarf off, then went into the hall. 'Mum?'

'Yes, darling—you're not ready! Where's your coat?'

'I've changed my mind. I've got a headache. I think I'll just lie down and read for a while.'

She started to undo her coat but her face reflected her disappointment. She wanted to be with Hugh, Woody realised. He reached out and stopped her as she struggled with the buttons. 'You go,' he told her. 'I'll be fine here by myself.'

She hesitated. 'Are you sure? What if you don't feel well?'

'Hugh will have his mobile. I've got the number. I'll call you—but, anyway, I'm fine. Please go. He's expecting you.'

She hesitated a moment, but then kissed him swiftly on the cheek and ran down the path. He closed the door softly behind her and turned to rest against it. It didn't matter. The fireworks were nothing.

He sighed heavily and went through to his bedroom, then booted up the chess programme. He'd see if he could get up to the next level. It knocked spots off trying to get on with Martin, and he was probably more likely to achieve it as well. . .

CHAPTER EIGHT

THE fireworks were wonderful, but Judith couldn't concentrate. She smiled and oohed and aahed with the others, but all she could think about was Edward and the fact that he was lying to her. Was it because of Martin? Were they really getting on so badly?

Oh, dear, she thought. They were thrust into each other's company without consultation, and perhaps their after-school arrangement, while suiting her and Hugh down to the ground, was not the best solution for the boys. Perhaps it would be better if Woody got off the school bus and walked home, and she could make a meal for the others, leave it for them and then cook again for herself and Woody when she got home.

Yes, that would be better.

'All right?'

Hugh's voice was soft in her ear, and she turned and tilted her head, giving him a bright smile over her shoulder. 'Yes, fine. You?'

He searched her face without replying. 'What is it?'

'What?'

'You're worried. What is it? Woody?'

Trust him to know there was something wrong. She sighed and leant against him. His body was hard and solid at her back, reassuring, and it felt so utterly right to be here with him like this with the children. If only Woody wasn't missing it would be like having a real family, but he *was* missing, and they *weren't a* real family—and she ought to remember that.

'Speak to me.'

She might have known he wouldn't give up, either.

124

She turned towards him. 'Yes, it's Woody. I don't know what to do about him. He's not getting on well with Martin. We've rather shoved them together. They're like chalk and cheese, poor kids.'

'Hmm. Have a chat with him and I'll talk to Martin. We'll liaise on Monday.'

'Maybe we need to rethink the after-school arrangement.'

'Maybe. We'll see—and you're missing all the fireworks.'

Her smile was a little strained. 'Not as many as Edward.'

'He could have come.'

'Perhaps he felt unwelcome.'

'Oh, Judith.' His arms came round her and hugged her, then turned her to face the fireworks again. As she turned she caught Martin's eye and in the second before he turned away she could almost feel his resentment in a physical wave.

Was he jealous of her relationship with his father? Was that possible?

Alice jiggled at her side. 'I can't see,' she complained, and Judith eased herself out of Hugh's arms and turned to him.

'Pick Alice up and put her on your shoulders,' she suggested.

'Want a ride, Toots?' he asked and, bending down, he tucked his head in between her legs and stood up again, raising her above the crowd. 'Better?'

'Oh, wow!' she exclaimed breathlessly. 'That's just excellent! I can see everything!'

Judith and Hugh exchanged grins, and then Judith caught another fulminating stare from Martin. Oh, dear, she thought, he really did resent her. On the pretext of avoiding Alice's dirty shoes Judith moved a little away from Hugh, and was relieved to see Martin's expresssion of satisfaction.

Oh, well, at least that had pleased him. She'd have to have a long talk with Woody to get to the bottom of this.

'Woody?'

She tapped on his bedroom door and opened it a crack. The light was still on, and it was no surprise to find her son locked in mortal combat with the computer.

He was playing chess, his face rapt with concentration—her presence unnoticed. Oh, well, she thought, he seemed happy enough now. There were no tears or tantrums—not that that was his style. She almost wished it was. Many disabled children screamed and ranted and worked their frustration out. Not Woody. He brooded on it, reasoned it out—dealt with it in a curiously adult and frighteningly composed way.

There were times when Judith would have given her eye teeth to see that composure crack and show the ordinary, vulnerable little boy inside. That she could have dealt with, hugging and loving and reassuring. This was so much harder, so much less accessible, and the older he grew the harder it became.

She went and made herself a cup of tea and curled up with it in front of the television. There was a film on which she had seen before. It was half way through but that didn't matter—she knew how it went, anyway. Besides, she wasn't really concentrating on the television so much as being available for when Woody emerged from his room.

It took nearly an hour, but finally he came into the sitting room and plonked himself down next to her, throwing her a victorious grin.

'I did it,' he said with satisfaction.

'Did what?'

'Got onto the next level in the chess programme.'

She returned the grin, delighted that he had finally achieved that particularly elusive goal. 'Well done. How are you feeling?'

'Fine.' He reddened slightly. 'Better.'

She sighed. 'Good.'

'How were the fireworks?'

'OK. Much as usual,' she lied. In fact, there had been one or two unusual ones he would have found fascinating, but she didn't think there was any great point in beating the issue to death. He'd missed them and that was that. More to the point was why. 'You should have come,' she added casually.

'Nah. Too noisy and crowded. Want another cup of tea?'

'Please.' She handed him her mug, watched him walk awkwardly through into the kitchen and then rested her head back against the wing of the sofa. So he wasn't going to discuss it. OK. She'd let it go—for now. Perhaps Al could get more out of him next weekend. Belle was happy to have him, he was pleased to go, Toots was off to her grandparents, and Martin to his rugby tour—and she and Hugh were off to a secret destination which Hugh refused to reveal.

'Just bring plenty of warm clothes,' he'd told her.

'Is it far?'

He'd shaken his head. 'Not very. A couple of hours in the car.'

From mid-Suffolk she calculated that could be Kent, well, any of the home counties, really—the Midlands, Humberside, the south coast—the choice was bewildering and she tried not to think about it too hard in case she was disappointed when they got there.

While Woody made the tea she closed her eyes and considered the options, and decided the South Downs would be wonderful. Hills, coast, quaint villages and bustling historic towns—perfect. Or Oxford, that most lovely of cities, set in gently rolling countryside peppered with stately homes and steeped in academia—which would be Hugh's choice?

Maybe Humberside, with the thrashing North Sea and winds straight off Siberia, and plenty of good reasons to stay in bed all day—

'Here.'

Her eyes flew open and soft colour brushed her cheeks. 'Thanks, Edward,' she murmured, taking her tea and banishing those particular images to the back of her mind. There would be plenty of time to indulge herself next weekend. . .

It was a funny old week. On Monday the radiographer was still finishing off at lunchtime, and so they were denied their secret tryst. Judith wouldn't have minded if she hadn't been feeling a little fragile, but she really badly wanted him to hold her and with Clare there it was impossible.

They took their coffee into the snug after they'd eaten and sat on the settee holding hands, and then jumped guiltily as Clare stuck her head round the door to tell them she was off.

From the knowing twinkle in her eye Judith realised that the woman had already worked out the extent of their relationship and so there was no point in trying to disguise it, but for the sake of the children they were keeping it under wraps for now.

The pitifully short remainder of their lunchbreak passed in a flurry of phone calls and one lingering, tender kiss that left them both screaming with frustration.

On Tuesday, of course, Hugh was at his children's clinic, and Judith went shopping and cleaned the flat and looked at her clothes and hoped to God that the hotel wasn't too smart because her clothes were really very ordinary and wouldn't stand up to much in the way of competition.

She sorted out skirts, blouses, a nice jumper and decent shoes for the hotel, and some jeans and warm woollies and walking boots in case Hugh had yomping in mind. She only had one coat that was warm enough, a navy blue wool reefer jacket which she had picked up in Oxfam for two pounds and after dry-cleaning had proved to be immaculate. That would have to do.

Then there were the undies. Oh, Lord, all her panties were decrepit and unflattering, her bras were serviceable and far from sexy and her nightdresses—well, how could you seduce anyone in a long T-shirt with little cats all over it?

She could always be outrageous, she thought, and wear nothing under her clothes and nothing to bed. That should warm the weekend up a touch!

She packed her case, shoved it under her bed and tried not to think about it.

On Wednesday she thought nothing would keep them apart, but then at ten-thirty there was a phone call from the wife of an old patient who had been treated in the past for migraine. He had had a recurrence and this time it refused to go away, and he'd been poleaxed by it now for nearly twenty-four hours. Could Hugh possibly fit him in?

Hugh being Hugh did so, of course, at lunchtime.

The man was brought in by his wife, almost prostrate with the severity of the headache—white as a sheet, his eyes tightly closed as she led him through into the consulting room.

Judith made their lunch just in case Hugh had time to eat it, and then was amazed forty minutes later when the patient emerged with his eyes open, still a little pale but vastly improved and extremely grateful.

'His temporal bone was locked solid. I just freed it,'

Hugh said in response to her questions about his miracle cure. 'He's easy. Not all migraines are caused by cranial dysfunction, though, so you have to treat as you find, of course. I know about him, though.'

He reached out and cupped her cheek. 'Judith?'

She looked up into his eyes longingly. 'It's been ages,' she murmured.

'I know—and tomorrow Clare will be here again, getting through a long list of X-rays, and on Friday I've fitted someone in at lunchtime because we're getting away at four and I didn't want to leave them over the weekend.' His fingers traced her jaw, then fell to her shoulder and drew her towards him.

She went into his arms and rested her head on his shoulder. Oh, how she needed to be held. On Monday evening Martin had been very uncommunicative and so had Woody, and she'd rushed him home as soon as she could, and tonight would no doubt be a repeat of the same fiasco.

'How's Woody's back been?' Hugh asked, as if he'd sensed the direction of her thoughts, one hand idly caressing her nape.

'Better now.'

'I'll have a look at him tonight. He's had a fortnight since I did any cranial work—I'd like to see if he's maintained the improvement.'

'He's moved up to the next level in the chess programme on the computer,' she told Hugh, 'so you obviously haven't managed to scramble his brain.'

He tutted. 'Such a lack of faith.' His hand slid from her nape down her back and round, cupping her breast gently. 'I want you,' he murmured. His body nudged hers and she squeezed her eyes tight shut and moaned softly.

'Don't,' she whispered. 'It just makes it worse.'

His laugh was short and frustrated. 'How can it? It's as bad as it can get already.'

She lifted her head and leant back, touching his face with her fingertips. 'Where are you taking me this weekend?' she asked.

'No. It's no use asking me in a weak moment. It's a surprise.'

She chewed her lip for a second, plucking up courage. 'Hugh, it's not anywhere too smart, is it?'

He hugged her. 'No. It's not smart, just cosy and quiet and very welcoming.'

She hardly dared ask the next question, but she had to for her peace of mind. 'Have you ever stayed there before? With a woman, I mean? Or Linda?'

His breath eased out on a sigh and he squeezed her gently. 'No. I've never taken another woman there for a weekend of unbridled passion. You are definitely the first. I've stayed there, yes, with the kids a few years ago, and again a few times since if I've attended conferences in that part of the world.'

'Which part?' she asked sneakily.

'No. Stop it. I'm not telling you.'

She laughed and pushed him away, infinitely happier now. 'You're such a tease.'

'Me?' His eyes were smouldering. 'You can talk, in that blouse that gapes every time you lean forwards a bit. If I catch one more glimpse of that smooth, soft breast I swear I'm going to rip your clothes off and make love to you no matter what.'

She blushed, her hands automatically going to the buttons to tug the blouse straight. 'You're not. Behave.'

'I am. And I've been behaving for days. The suspense is killing me.'

Judith was so glad she wasn't alone. Her burning need to be next to him, to shed the trappings of civilisation and be at one with the man she loved was almost overwhelming. Roll on the weekend, she thought fervently.

*   *   *

'Are you sure you'll be all right?'

Woody wrapped her awkwardly in his arms and hugged her. 'Of course I'll be all right. You know where I'll be. I'll be fine with Al.'

'You've got the mobile number?'

He grinned wickedly. 'I've got the number and name and address of the hotel as well, but I'm not telling you.'

Judith straightened and stared at him in amazement. 'What? He's told you?'

'Only so I could contact you in an emergency.'

'And you won't tell me?'

'Nope.'

'You rat.' She hugged him, delighted that he and Hugh were getting on so well and that Woody would keep a secret like that and not break Hugh's trust—even if it was infuriating! 'Do try and get some sleep—don't chat all night, will you?'

'I expect we'll watch 18-rated movies all night and then go out and rape a few old ladies—'

'Stop teasing,' she laughed, swatting him round the shoulders. 'You're so wicked. Go on, then, or you'll miss the bus. I'll pick you up on Sunday.'

She watched him go, checked her case again and wondered how Hugh was gettting on with Martin and Toots. What was he telling them about the weekend? She and Hugh had been so busy they hadn't really had time to discuss it, but she had a feeling they didn't know that she and Hugh were going away together. Would Martin mind? Oh, Lord. . .

'That's *our* hotel,' Martin said belligerently. 'Why are you taking *her* there?'

Hugh sighed and stifled his frustration. 'Because it's a nice place. Because I fancy a weekend away, just walking around in the hills, and I didn't want to go on my own.'

'You just want to get in her knickers,' Martin said with disgust.

Hugh was spared the indignity of responding to that barbed remark by Alice's arrival in the kitchen. 'Will Grannie make me a cake, do you suppose?' she asked, skipping and bouncing round the table.

'I expect so. Are you looking forward to it?'

'Yes, it'll be brilliant. Will you be all right without us, though?'

Hugh hugged her. 'Of course I will. Judith and I are going away, too, remember. We're all going to have fun.'

Martin snorted pointedly, turned his back on his father and stood at the window, glowering down the garden. It was a wonder the trees didn't wither and die, Hugh thought, under the malevolence in that glare. He couldn't leave the remark unanswered, but on the other what could he say? Yes, you're right, I do want to get in her knickers and I already have, furthermore, and it was incredible? Don't be absurd, why would I want to do a thing like that? It's none of your business? Which?

The truth, of course, although in rather more subtle language, because Hugh had always brought them up to know the truth. But this was the first time his sexuality had been challenged by his son and he found it difficult in the extreme. If it hadn't been for the problem of Martin's relationship with Woody it would have been much easier to address, of course, but the boys really seemed to have such a fragile truce—if one existed at all—that Hugh was quite at a loss.

And so he said nothing because, apart from anything else, Toots was leaping about and clamouring for his attention and they were going to be late for school in a minute and he just didn't have time to deal with it now.

He arrived back from the school run late for his first patient, and that set the tone for the entire day. By the time they shut the doors at four thirty, half an hour late, they were both run ragged.

'We could just stay here,' Judith suggested, only half joking.

'No. Come on, we're going now. Is your bag ready for the car?'

She nodded.

'Right, let's hit the road. I wanted to get away sooner to avoid the traffic—it's always hell on Fridays.'

'Where are we going?'she asked yet again.

He grinned. 'Surprise.

'I'll know sooner or later.'

'I'll keep you guessing.'

He threw their cases in the boot of his car, set the burglar alarm and locked the house, then they were off. She settled back against the comfortable leather upholstery, folded her hands in her lap and possessed her soul in patience. Damn the man, he wasn't going to tell her so she'd just keep quiet and say nothing. That would irritate him!

'Judith?' The hand on her arm was gentle but insistent. 'Judith, wake up, we're here.'

She opened her eyes, sat up and stretched a little. A little sleepy 'Oh,' escaped her, and she turned to him and smiled apologetically. 'I'm sorry. I meant to stay awake and talk to you, but it's been such a busy day.'

He chuckled and leant forwards, dropping a light kiss on her dry lips. She flicked her tongue out to moisten them and he groaned softly and turned back to the wheel, resting his head on it.

'I promised myself I wasn't going to attack you the moment we arrived,' he muttered, 'but you'd drive a monk crazy.' He lifted his head, gave her a rueful grin and opened the door. 'Come on, let's go in.'

She got out of the car and looked up at the hotel. It

was long and low and thatched, quaintly pretty in the floodlights, and very welcoming. She didn't have a clue where it was.

'Aren't you going to ask?' he murmured from behind her.

'It isn't really relevant,' she told him, meaning it. 'We're here, and we're together, and it could be on the moon for all the difference it would make.'

He chuckled and ushered her towards the entrance. Feeling sleepy and crumpled and not really smart enough for a hotel, she walked hesitantly through the door and instantly forgot about her appearance.

The room they entered was fairly large, heavily beamed and charming. There was a log fire crackling lazily in the hearth, two retrievers were stretched out asleep in front of it and a couple dressed in casual clothes dozed on the settee nearby.

Behind the reception desk was a middle-aged woman in a pretty jumper and leggings, perched on a stool chatting to a young man over the desk, and as they went in she took one look at Hugh then jumped up and came round to envelop him in a hug. 'Hello, Hugh,' she said warmly. 'Oh, it is good to see you again—I thought you'd deserted us!'

'No. Just busy. Pam, I'd like you to meet Judith, a friend of mine. Judith, this is Pam Verey—she and her husband Stan run the hotel.'

Pam turned her searching brown eyes on Judith and scanned her face, then a lovely welcoming smile broke out over her soft features and she reached out a hand. 'Hello—I'm very pleased to meet you.'

And pleased, Judith thought, that Hugh had a 'friend' after all this time. She knew immediately that Hugh hadn't lied to her and that he'd never brought a woman here. She also realised that for him to have brought her and introduced her to Pam was significant in itself.

If she'd needed any further proof that she wasn't just an idle diversion, this was surely it.

Pam turned to the young man. 'Danny, take these two up to their room, could you, love? And hurry back down, now, won't you, Hugh, because Stan's venison casserole is on tonight and it's going like there's no tomorrow. I'd hate you to miss it. I'll save you the table by the window. Up you go. Danny'll take your luggage.'

They followed the obligingly laden Danny up a set of narrow, twisting stairs and down a corridor to the door at the end. He put the cases down, swung the door open and put the cases on the rack, then left them to it.

The door closed with a quiet click, and Hugh reached for her.

'What about the venison casserole?' Judith murmured.

'What about it? I need to hold you.'

She pushed him away gently. 'And I need a shower and a change of clothes and something to eat.'

'You're boring,' he said with a laugh, 'but probably right.' He stripped off his jacket and hung it over the back of a chair, then sat down on the end of the bed, drawing her attention to it for the first time.

Oak, with heavy barleytwist posts and pretty curtains, it was a real antique four-poster, utterly in keeping with the heavily beamed walls and ceiling and the sloping floor and atticky ceiling of the delightful room.

'This is really beautiful,' she murmured, looking round.

'Lovely, isn't it? The whole place is like this, but I asked for the most private room.'

'*En suite?*'

'Of course. The bathroom must be through that door.'

She opened the door and found a gleaming white suite in a Victorian design tucked in under the eaves. There was a shower over the bath, with a shower spray like an old fashioned telephone, and heavy brass cross-head taps that conjured the feel of the era.

It was the attention to detail that made it all work so well, Judith thought as she stood under the shower spray a few minutes later. That and plenty of hot water and efficient central heating—

'What—?'

'Shh. I need a shower, too.'

'But—'

'Shh.' His mouth cut off her protests, and seconds later she was in his arms. 'I want you,' he said unnecessarily.

She needed no persuading. She had to wash and dry her hair, though, before supper because they had ended up under the full force of the water, oblivious to the drenching spray—lost in another world.

'At least we'll be able to concentrate on our food,' Hugh said with a chuckle as they dressed.

'If there's any left.'

'There'll be plenty. There always is.'

Judith's stomach rumbled and she laughed, holding it. 'I hope so. I'm starving.'

They went back down to be greeted by Pam who showed them to their table. As she had promised she'd saved them the one by the window so they could see the floodlit garden, and she had also put some of Stan's casserole on one side in case they should want it.

It was delicious. By the time they had waded through the huge helping and done justice to the sweet trolley they were unable to face the cheese and biscuits.

'Coffee by the fire?' Pam suggested.

They looked at each other questioningly. The urgency to be alone was gone, their desire slaked for now, and the thought of sitting by the fire appealed to Judith's hopelessly romantic soul.

'That sounds lovely,' she said to Hugh.

He turned to Pam with a smile. 'Yes, please, that would be wonderful.'

They settled themselves on the settee where another

couple had dozed earlier, their feet stretched out towards the fire, and the dogs thumped their tails once in welcome and carried on the serious business of sleeping off their supper.

Pam brought the coffee over to them and set it down, complete with a tray of very dark, thin mint crisps which were Judith's absolute favourite and which she hadn't tasted for years.

'Going for a walk on the Downs in the morning?' she asked Hugh, and Judith laughed softly and bit into a mint.

'Did I say something funny?' Pam asked, looking confused.

'No. I kept our destination a secret, and Judith slept all the way here. She didn't know where we were.'

'And I gave it away.'

She looked remorseful, and Hugh laughed. 'Forget it. This place was the surprise, not the area.'

'Oh, but the Downs are wonderful!'

'And so are you and your hotel.'

Pam flapped a hand dismissively at him, but Judith could see she was touched and pleased by his praise. She left them alone then, and Judith turned to Hugh.

'So, are we?'

'Going for a walk? If you like.'

'Let's see what the weather's like.'

'Mmm. If we're lucky it'll be awful and we can have a lie-in.'

The message in his eyes was unmistakable.

'Sounds interesting,' Judith murmured.

'Oh, you don't know the half of it.' His finger traced a pattern on the back of her hand. 'All we've really done is whet our appetites. We've never even got beyond the first course.'

'And now?'

His eyes burned into hers, and he held one of the tempting little chocolates up to her lips. 'Now we're going to go for the whole menu, right through to the after dinner mints.'

She took the mint from his fingers and he licked the trace of chocolate from them in a blatantly sensuous gesture that left her weak and trembling. 'Hugh. . .'

'Come on.'

He stood up, pulled her to her feet and ushered her up the stairs and along to their room. Once through the door he hung the 'Do Not Disturb' notice on the knob, closed it firmly and reached for her.

He'd been right. They hadn't even scratched the surface, and yet curiously the most wonderful thing about their love-making was the lack of haste—the time to savour every touch, to linger here and there and tease a little. And then the luxury of being able to lie together and sleep—instead of rushing downstairs to deal with the afternoon patients—made Judith realise just how lacking their relationship had been until now.

Those snatched moments, although infinitely precious to them, were just the tip of the iceberg. There was so much more to savour, so much more to give, to receive, to share.

They made love lazily all night and again when they woke, then—after a leisurely breakfast at an indecently late hour—they walked for miles along the South Downs in the bracing wind and glorious autumn sunshine, returning to the hotel in time for tea and scones by the fire and another shared shower before coming down again for dinner.

And then, sitting by the fire with their coffee and the dogs, Hugh seemed preoccupied. She waited and after a moment he picked up her hand and held it, looking down at it as he stroked it thoughtfully.

'There's something I want to discuss with you,' he murmured and, looking up, he met her eyes.

He's afraid, she realised suddenly, and her mouth felt

dry and her heart began to race. This is goodbye, she thought. He's going to tell me that it's all over—

'I love you,' he said softly, cutting off her skittering thoughts at a stroke. 'You must know that—it's been obvious for weeks. What's been less obvious with the problems we're having with the boys is whether we can make a go of our relationship, but I really want to try. This weekend with you has proved to me beyond any doubt that we belong together. The very thought of living without you makes me sick with dread.

'I want to marry you, Judith. I want to go to bed with you at night and wake up with you in the morning. I want to have babies with you and plan a future together and know that you'll be there for me.'

He looked down, his thumb idly brushing the back of her hand. 'What I don't know is how the boys will react, or if you think we'll be able to work round their fears and problems. Whatever, I'm not letting you go out of my life and, if that's what it takes, we'll carry on like this until the boys leave home and then we'll be together, but I can't live without you.'

'Oh, Hugh. . .' Her eyes filled and splashed over, and with a muffled cry she threw herself into his arms.

'I take it that's a yes,' he murmured, and she laughed and sniffed and lifted her head. There was a silly smile plastered all over her face, but she didn't care. 'Of course it's a yes—and the boys will be fine. We'll talk to them and reason with them, and work things out. Oh, Hugh, I love you so much—'

She threw herself back into his arms, and they wrapped round her and hugged her so tight she couldn't even breathe.

When he finally let her go he called Pam and asked for a bottle of champagne.

'Celebrating something?' she asked with a knowing smile.

'Judith's agreed to marry me,' Hugh told her, and the next second all hell broke loose.

Pam hugged him, Stan came out of the kitchen and was slapping him on the back and giving Judith great smacking kisses, and the champagne flowed and everybody was laughing.

The euphoria lasted almost twenty-four hours—until Judith walked round to Al's to pick Woody up.

Belle opened the door, a worried look on her face, and took her to one side. 'This Martin boy,' she began. 'He's a real problem, Judith. He's bullying your son, you know. I heard him talking to Al in the night. They thought I was asleep. Martin calls him Spaz and Twiglet and things like that, and he really seems to have got under Woody's skin. You've really got to talk to them both, you know, Judith. It's the first time I've ever known Woody cry.'

'Cry? He was crying?'

The bubble burst, and Judith felt her euphoria draining away. 'Oh, damn.'

'I'm sorry, but I thought you ought to know. Anyway, how was your weekend?'

Judith looked at her miserably. 'Wonderful. He asked me to marry him—and I can't, can I? Not now.'

CHAPTER NINE

BROACHING the subject with Hugh was going to be tricky, Judith realised. It was one thing for her to say the boys were having trouble forming a relationship but it was quite another for her to accuse Hugh's son of bullying, especially without any direct evidence.

And evidence, of course, she didn't have. When she had tried to discuss it with Woody over breakfast on Monday morning he refused to comment on Belle's report, saying she had misunderstood or misheard.

'So you weren't crying?'

Woody couldn't look at her, always a bad sign. 'Not much. I was just feeling a bit low—missing you, I suppose. It's no big deal.'

'It is to me.'

'No.' He leant across from his chair and squeezed her hand briefly. 'Really, Mum, it's OK. Did you have a good weekend with Hugh?'

Thank God he wasn't still looking at her, because she felt her cheeks scald with heat. 'Yes, it was lovely. The hotel was very pretty—a thatched Tudor house with lots of beams. Heaps of character.'

'Good. I'm glad you enjoyed it. You deserved a holiday.' He looked at his watch and lurched to his feet, grabbing his bag. 'I'm going to miss the bus—see you later. Oh, by the way, Al said I could go round there after school tonight so I'll be at theirs when you finish work, OK?'

And he went out of the door without waiting for an answer.

She cleared the table thoughtfully, then made her way

round the corner to Hugh's house. He was just back from the school run as she arrived, and she was hardly over the threshold before he swept her into his arms, hugged her close and pressed his face into her hair.

'I missed you so much last night,' he murmured. 'Let's get married at the end of the week. If we get a special licence—'

'Hugh, we can't.'

He hugged her again, laughter lacing his words. 'Oh, all right, we'll do it the week after if you insist.'

She eased back a little in his arms, tipped her head back and met his eyes. They were brimming over with love and happiness, and deep inside her chest a great aching void was starting to form. 'I meant we can't get married.'

His arms dropped and he stared at her in silence for a moment. 'What do you mean, we can't get married?' he asked eventually. 'Oh, Lord, you mean it, don't you? What's happened?'

She didn't mean to cry. She really was going to be sensible and deal with this in a rational manner, but the gentleness in his voice and the concern in his eyes were her undoing. She squeezed her lids shut, clamped her lips over the wrenching sobs and fell into his arms.

'Oh, Judith, sweetheart, it's all right. Hush now. Come on. Talk to me.'

She tried, she really did, but the words were all dammed up behind the sobs and they had to be got out of the way first.

He led her into the kitchen, pulled her onto his lap on the sofa and held her until the storm quietened a little. Then he wiped her eyes, told her to blow her nose and then ordered her, very gently, to tell him what had happened.

'It's the boys,' she began, and then the tears welled up again.

Hugh sighed. 'Of course. When isn't it? What is it this time?'

She sniffed, pulling the soggy tissue apart and shredding it absently all over her lap. 'Apparently Al's mother overheard them talking. Woody won't tell me anything, but she says he told Al that Martin—well, he seems to be calling him names and things—'

'What names?'

She shredded the tissue some more. 'Twiglet and—well, Spaz—that sort of thing.' She lifted a shoulder in a helpless gesture.

Hugh's mouth was a grim line. 'I've had this conversation with him once already. I thought I'd got through to him. Obviously not. I'll have another go.'

'Hugh, don't make it worse,' she pleaded. 'Woody's spending more time with Al now, and I thought it would be better if I just cook for you and go when surgery's finished. Then you only need to see Woody if you treat him, and they won't be thrust into each other's company all the time.'

'I still need to speak to him—and, regardless, this relationship of ours is coming out into the open, Judith. I'm not sneaking around feeling guilty any more. If I want to spend time with you I will, and if we want to go away together we will, and if the kids don't want to be together that's their problem.

'We both need and deserve a little personal space and, frankly, sneaking around at lunchtime, stealing ten minutes together, isn't on. It's not enough. I want more from you, darling, much more, and I'm going to make sure we have it—and ultimately we are going to get married, even if we have to wait years. OK?'

She nodded, relieved that he had taken the implied criticism of his son so well. She might have known he would, being the sort of person he was, but people could be irrational about their children. Apparently not Hugh, though. She knew he would talk to Martin, and she also knew that that talk would probably lead to even greater animosity towards her, but the problem had to be addressed. She just hoped Hugh managed to remain calm. . .

'Oh, come on, Dad, it was just a joke!'

'A joke?' Hugh felt a muscle in his jaw twitch, and forced himself to relax. 'Martin, I don't think calling someone with cerebral palsy "Spaz" says a great deal about your sense of humour—or your common decency.'

Martin rolled his eyes. 'Are you about to go into the I'm glad your mother isn't alive to see you routine now?'

Hugh closed his eyes. He wasn't glad Linda wasn't alive. No matter that he had now found happiness with Judith, there was no way he could ever be glad Linda wasn't alive. But that she shouldn't have to see Martin like this—yes, he was glad. Glad because, apart from anything else, he felt he must have failed them both.

He tried again. 'Look, Martin, just try and put yourself in Edward's shoes for a moment. How would you feel if someone called you Spaz and then tried to pass it off as a joke?'

Martin flushed and squirmed, to Hugh's great relief. He was beginning to think the child had no compassion in him at all, but apparently he had.

'I didn't mean to hurt him. It's just that he's—weird, you know?'

'He makes you feel uncomfortable, doesn't he?'

'Mmm. I think it's just being shoved together so much. I'm not ready for it.'

Hugh felt guilty for imposing his own needs on his son and throwing the two boys together. 'I know. Still, it won't happen any more. Now I'm not treating him so often he's going to go straight home after school and

Judith will leave when I close the surgery, except on the days when I treat him.'

'So Judith won't eat with us either?'

Hugh shook his head. 'No.'

A flicker of something that could have been relief darted through Martin's eyes and was gone. 'Oh.'

'But I will be seeing her occasionally after work, and we'll be spending time together at weekends.'

Martin's face became shuttered. 'Do I need to know this?' he asked indifferently.

Hugh sighed. 'I thought you might be interested.'

'In your sex life? Nope, not really.'

Hugh reined his temper in with difficulty and tried to remember how hard this must be for his son. 'I'm not talking about my sex life,' he said with forced calm.

'I'm so glad because I really don't want to hear about it. Can I go and get on with my homework now?' Martin asked.

Hugh sighed again and let him go. The situation with Woody was far from resolved, but if everyone could step back a little and cool down maybe things would settle to the point where they could reintroduce negotiations—and perhaps with time he could convince his son that his relationship with Judith was about more than just sex.

Just at the moment, though, his feelings for her were too new, too private, too vulnerable to drag out into the open and discuss with the angry teenager his son had turned into. How could he talk about love and sharing and soul-mates with someone hell-bent on reducing every emotion to its most basic component?

He stabbed his hands through his hair and sighed. He needed to talk to her, to share this with her, to discuss ways of dealing with it. He just wanted to be with her all the time, starting now. Impatient and impulsive—traits he shared with his son—Hugh found playing a waiting game impossibly difficult.

The next day was Tuesday, his children's clinic day, and it would be Wednesday before he could be with her again.

It seemed like a life sentence. . .

On Thursday afternoon Woody turned up without warning, arriving just minutes before Martin and Alice were due to get back. As he walked in Judith knew there was something wrong.

'What is it?' she asked him, jumping to her feet and crossing to him with swift, anxious strides. 'Edward, how did you get that bruise? Has someone hit you?' She turned him to the light and clucked worriedly.

He took her hand and moved it away from his chin. 'Nobody hit me. It happened at the RDA—'

'Did you fall off?'

'Uh-uh. Pipkin threw his head up and smashed me in the face. Something startled him.'

She stood back, her panic receding a little, and eyed him searchingly. 'Your neck's crooked.'

'I know. It crunched disgustingly, and now I can't move my head round to the right and my shoulders are all uneven.'

She sighed and patted his arm. 'Go into the kitchen and get a drink and a biscuit, and I'll tell Hugh. There's some cake in the tin as well, I think.'

She watched him go, then a moment later Hugh emerged.

'Problems?' he murmured.

'He's been barged by a pony. He's got a bruise on his chin and his neck crunched. He can't turn his head.'

Hugh nodded and disappeared down the corridor after Woody, leaving her to make the patient's next appointment. She popped her head round the kitchen door when she had finished.

'Do you want me to show Mrs Barrett in, or are you going to do Woody?'

Hugh shook his head. 'No, I'll do him when I've finished. I'll have more time then. He can lie down in the snug until then and relax a bit—it's very tense. I'm coming now. Woody, go and put your feet up in front of the television.'

Judith went back and showed Mrs Barrett into the consulting room, greeted another patient who had arrived early and waved hello to Martin and Alice as they arrived. A few minutes later the children went through to the snug, armed with cake and drinks and a packet of biscuits.

'Mind you don't ruin your appetites,' she warned, but her words fell on deaf ears. The door shut with a decisive little bang, and she pulled a face. 'Consider yourself told to mind your own business,' she mumbled under her breath. There were raised voices for a second or two, and then quiet except for the television.

She went into the kitchen, put the finishing touches to the evening meal and went back just as Hugh finished with the last patient.

'Do you want to eat first or treat Woody?' she asked him.

'Is there enough for all of us?'

She thought of the casserole. 'No, not really. I could do extra potatoes and carrots.'

'Well, why don't you do that, anyway? I'll treat him now and then we'll all have supper together.'

He opened the door of the snug, and she heard a muttered exclamation before the door closed. While she was dealing with the last patient she could hear raised voices and then, just as she closed the front door, the snug door burst open and Martin flounced out and ran upstairs.

Seconds later Hugh emerged with Woody, red-faced and embarrassed.

'What's going on?' she asked, eyeing her son's heightened colour with concern.

'Martin wanted the settee—he kicked Woody off.'

'It doesn't matter—'

'It does. I wanted you lying down without having to carry the weight of your head. It was part of your treatment. He had no right to interfere.'

'I don't suppose he saw it like that,' Woody protested. 'I was in his place—I'm always in his place.'

Hugh's mouth tightened. 'That's no excuse to be rude to a guest.'

'But I'm not a guest, am I? I'm just a pain.' Hugh opened his mouth to protest but Woody waved him down. 'I understand how he feels, Hugh. It is his house.'

Judith swallowed. How could Woody be so mature and reasoned and sensible about it and Martin be so defensive? Would they ever be able to resolve their differences?

She met Hugh's eyes over Woody's head and saw the despair and frustration she felt echoed in their cobalt depths. 'Come on, Woody,' he said gently, and rested a hand lightly on Edward's shoulder as he ushered him into the consulting room and closed the door with a quiet click.

'So,' Hugh said, settling himself down at the head of the treatment table and taking Woody's neck in his hands. 'I gather your friend Pipkin's responsible for this little crisis.'

Woody grinned lopsidedly. 'Yeah. We decided it was called horsteopathy.'

Hugh chuckled. 'Horsteopathy, eh? Well, may I make a suggestion? Go for the traditional treatment in future.'

Woody gave a wheezy chuckle. 'I think so. Apart from anything else, I thought he'd knocked my teeth out.'

'Hmm.' Hugh released the tight coloumn of the boy's neck and looked at his jaw. 'Open your mouth and close it—well, it's moving OK. I think you might have been lucky. I'll just free your neck off and then I'll have a go at your head—I expect your temporal bone might have locked again after a thump like that.'

He stretched and pulled, easing out the tension in the neck muscles. Once he was satisfied with the soft tissues he freed the joint with a well-placed twist and straightened the boy up again. 'How's that feel?'

'Better. I can really feel the difference.'

'Good. Now, about this head.'

He rested his fingers lightly on Woody's scalp over the sutures between the skull bones, and closed his eyes. The rhythm was good, he thought after a moment as he tuned in to the subtle movements. Much better than before, and the bones were still moving freely. He'd been lucky that his neck joint seemed to have taken most of the force of the blow and that his jaw and skull were unaffected.

He worked with the rhythm for a few minutes, boosting the flow of cerebrospinal fluid and checking that there were no areas of turbulence because of the neck injury. Once he was happy it was moving well he settled the flow down again and stopped.

'OK?' he asked Woody.

The boy nodded. 'Great. Thanks. I hope you didn't mind me coming over like this.'

'Of course I didn't mind, Woody. You're always welcome, whether you've got a problem or not.'

His smile was wry. 'Perhaps not always,' he replied.

He hesitated, chewing his lip in a gesture so like his mother's that Hugh felt a lump in his throat. Lord, he loved this kid.

'I just wanted to say I'm really glad Mum's got you for a friend. She's done so much for me—given up everything. She could have had a career, got married—all sorts of things—but she gave it all up to give her time to me. I'm really glad for her that she's got someone to make up for that a bit.' He floundered to a halt, embarrassed by his long speech, and Hugh could have hugged him.

Instead, he put a hand on Woody's shoulder and squeezed gently. 'Thanks, Edward. She's a very special person, you know, your mum.'

'Yeah, I know.'

He patted the skinny shoulder under his hand. 'Come on, she's got supper for us.'

A look of panic flared in Woody's eyes in the second before his lids dropped. 'OK,' he said, but Hugh could see that it wasn't and wished now he hadn't suggested it.

Judith, though, had got there before him. 'I've left the casserole on the hob for you,' she said as they emerged. 'I think, if you don't mind, I'll take Edward home now. He could do with a rest and I've got a stack of ironing I've been putting off.'

He fought against the urge to protest, and also cut off the suggestion that he should come round later and spend an hour or so with her that evening.

Let it rest, he cautioned himself. Give them all time. He forced a smile. 'OK. Thanks. I'll see you in the morning.'

He watched them go, and with a sigh he turned and went back into the kitchen. He couldn't face another row with Martin, he decided. He'd try a little icy disapproval instead and see if that worked. Really, the boy's behaviour was getting worse by the minute. Got any ideas, Linda? he asked the ether. He's your son, too. Pity he didn't take after you.

Alice was sitting at the kitchen table, making patterns with salt on her table mat. 'Look, Daddy, it's a dog,' she told him. He went over and looked at the mess.

'Where?'

She sighed patiently. 'Here are its eyes, and here are its ears, and that's its nose—can you see it now?'

He gave her a weak smile. 'Yes, darling. It's a lovely dog.'

She plonked her finger randomly in the salt, then sat

back with a grin. 'It's a Dalmatian,' she announced cheer-fully, her grin lighting up the kitchen.

She took after her mother, Hugh thought fondly. Happy, carefree, generous-natured—why couldn't he have had two like that? He loved Martin desperately, but there were times when he didn't understand what made him tick.

'Oh, hell,' he muttered.

'Daddy! That was naughty!'

He grinned weakly. 'Sorry, Toots. Can you clear your Dalmatian up, please, so we can have supper, and then go and call Martin down from his bedroom?'

She carried the mat to the sink, only losing half of the salt to the floor *en route*, then skipped out.

'Martin!' she yelled from the bottom of the stairs.

'Go and get him, Toots—don't yell,' Hugh said mildly.

There was a thundering of little feet up the first flight of stairs, then she yelled again.

'I'm coming, for God's sake!' Martin bellowed from the attic, and Hugh sighed and stared down the darkened garden. Kids, he thought. Why was it all such an uphill struggle?

The door was hurled back and bounced off the wall. 'Have Punch and Judy gone?'

Hugh gritted his teeth. 'Yes. Jud*ith* had things to do.'

'Good. All the more for us—that smells good. Is there plenty? I'm starving.'

'There's plenty,' Hugh said, looking into the pot. There was. There would have been quite enough for Judith and Woody to have stayed.

'I wish they were here. They're never here now any more,' Toots said with an elaborate sigh. 'I like Woody. He reads to me, and he lets me sit on his lap.'

She gave Martin a pointed stare which he ignored. 'And I like Judith,' she continued, beating the subject to death. 'I think she's pretty, and she cooks lovely food for us. I wish I could have her for a mummy.'

Hugh was flummoxed. Should he say anything?

'Look,' Martin said with elaborate disdain, 'it's bad enough to have them here all the time. Do we really have to talk about them even when they're not?'

Toots pouted. 'You're horrid. You just don't like Woody 'cos he's better'n you at chess.'

Martin half rose, but Hugh pushed him gently back into his chair. 'All right, Toots, that's enough. Let's change the subject.'

Was it true? Was Martin jealous of Woody? Lord, kids were so complicated.

'So, how was school today?' he asked with forced cheer, and dragged the conversation kicking and screaming off the subject of the woman he loved and her son who was fast stealing what was left of his heart. . .

Judith looked at the envelope with a mixture of dread and confusion. Why was her mother writing to her? She never wrote to her. She always sent Christmas and birthday cards, but often Judith just threw them out. There were too many painful memories, too much emotion tied up in their relationship for her to forget it.

She stuffed the letter into her bag, waved Woody off and went round the corner to Hugh's. He wasn't back from the school run yet so she let herself in and went into the kitchen, put the kettle on and then reluctantly pulled the letter out.

She stared at the envelope for some time, as if she would glean some idea of the contents from the outside, then with trembling fingers she tore it open and pulled the letter out.

It was a single sheet, its message bare and to the point.

'Dear Judith, Your father has had a stroke and would like to see you. He is in Ipswich Hospital. Please come. Mum.'

She laid the letter down on the kitchen table and smoothed it out, her fingers shaking. A stroke. Her mother didn't say how bad, but if he was asking for her presumably it wasn't that bad. The words blurred, and she blinked. Ipswich. That was only half an hour away by train. Perhaps she could ask Al's mother to have Woody tomorrow so she could go.

No. What had they done for her? Why should she go? Had they been there when she'd needed them?

The back door opened and shut, and then Hugh was there, pulling her into his arms. 'Morning, gorgeous,' he murmured, tipping her face up for a kiss, then he stopped in shock and stared at her face.

'Lord, darling, what's happened? You look as if you've seen a ghost.'

She pushed the letter towards him, and he picked it up and scanned the few short lines.

'Oh, hell, sweetheart, I'm sorry. Do you want to borrow the car?'

She blinked up at him in astonishment. 'Why would I want to borrow the car? I can't drive.'

'To go to him. Blast. If I didn't have so many patients today I'd take you—perhaps we can reschedule the afternoon patients. Have you looked at the book?'

She waved a hand at him. 'Whoa, Hugh, slow down. I'm not going.'

He stopped on his way to the door and looked at her incredulously, then crossed the kitchen slowly to her side again. 'Not going?' he echoed. 'But he's your father.'

'Yes—and when I needed him he threw me out.'

Hugh stabbed his hand through his hair and gave a heavy sigh. 'OK, so he behaved badly—does that mean you have to as well?'

Judith pulled a chair out from the table and sat down in it with a plonk. 'You really think I should go? Despite all they said and did, you think I should drop everything and rush over there hotfoot just because he crooks his little finger?'

Hugh shook his head. 'No. I think you should do it because you love him and it may be your last chance to tell him that.'

'Oh, God.' She covered her mouth with her hand to trap the sob but it wouldn't be held in, and the next moment she was in his arms on his lap, cradled against his chest while she cried like a baby.

Finally she hiccupped to a halt, and he mopped her up and hugged her. 'You do love him, don't you?' he said gently.

She nodded miserably. 'He's my father.'

'So go to him. Maybe it's time to heal the wounds, Judith. Fourteen years is a long time.'

She sniffed and nodded. 'Perhaps tomorrow. I'll go down on the train if Belle can have Woody.'

'Marty's spending the day with Colin. Why don't I take you down, and Toots and Woody and I can mooch around Ipswich and find something to do while you visit him, and then if you think he's up to it Woody could see him, too.'

She shook her head. 'He doesn't like disability. He's like Martin—it makes him uncomfortable. I don't think Woody needs any more of that at the moment.'

'Never mind. We'll find something to entertain us, I have no doubt, and Alice will be over the moon having her hero to herself.'

'Her hero?'

'Woody. She thinks he's wonderful.'

Judith smiled wanly. 'So do I. I just wish I could convince him he is. He's got a lousy self-image.'

'And Martin's done nothing for it,' Hugh said flatly. 'I'm sorry.'

She hugged him. 'It's not your fault. They'll sort themselves out in the end.'

'They'll have to. I meant what I said, Judith. We're getting married come hell or high water, even if we have to wait five years.'

'Five years is a long time, Hugh.'

'Not as long as a lifetime without you.'

She turned her face up to his. 'No. No, you're right. I'd just like to have their blessing, that's all.'

His smile was wry. 'I think we have to be realistic. Woody's happy for us to spend time together so long as he's left out of the equation, but I'm beginning to think you're as much of a problem for Martin as Woody is. I think he's jealous of you.'

'Do you think he feels I'm taking Linda's place?' she mused.

'Maybe. Whatever, I hope we can sort it out soon because I'd like us all to be together for Christmas—that is, if you haven't got any other plans.'

Plans? She had no plans. She never had plans for Christmas. She and Woody spent it alone together, in front of the television, and if things were good they had nuts and chocolates and other goodies to nibble during the afternoon and evening. But plans?

'No, we've got no plans.'

'Would you like to join us?'

She gave him a teasing smile while she stalled. 'You just want your dinner cooked,' she said.

'No. No strings. I'll do it all, I promise. I just want to treat you, and spend time with you—be a family.' His eyes were filled with longing, and his voice had a wistful note which she found it impossible to resist.

'We could ask them, I suppose,' she said doubtfully.

'They'll be fine. One day, Judith. Even Martin can manage one day.'

She smiled at him. He was right, it was only one day. Of course the boys could cope with it.

She just wished she had Hugh's confidence. . .

CHAPTER TEN

JUDITH wouldn't have recognised her father if it hadn't been for her mother sitting beside him. He looks so old, she thought with shock, his wonderful, thick dark hair white now and less abundant, and his face thinner and so pale.

Guilt tugged at her but she shook it aside, drew a steadying breath and walked quietly up to the bed, the flowers dangling forgotten from her hand.

'Hello, Dad, Mum.'

'Judith!' Marion Wright's voice was hushed with shock, and she jumped to her feet and hugged her daughter. 'Oh, darling, you came. I'm so glad. Look, Edward, it's Judith!'

Her father looked at her with eyes faded by age and illness, and then reached out his hand. 'Jude?' he murmured. 'Oh, Jude—'

His voice cracked and he pulled her towards him so that she lost her balance and sat down on the bed, leaning against him and finding her arms quite naturally sliding round him to hug his body. The flowers fell unheeded to the floor. He still felt the same, she thought, even if he looked older. He still felt like her father. . .

She heard him sobbing, and then she wasn't sure if it was him or herself, or both. Oh, it felt so good to be held by him again. She'd missed him unbearably, missed his love and approval and support.

She sat up, dashing the tears from her cheeks, and looked at him. 'What a pair of wet weekends we are,' she said, dredging up a smile. She retrieved the mangled flowers from the floor and handed them to him. 'Here, these are for you. I'm afraid they've got a bit squashed.'

He took them and laid them on the bed, then reached for her hand again, clearly more interested in her than her flowers.

'It's really you,' he murmured, and touched her cheek with shaking fingers.

'Of course it's me,' she assured him with a smile. 'A bit older, maybe a bit wiser, but me just the same.' She straightened and looked searchingly at him. 'So, what have you been doing to yourself?'

He flapped his hand. 'Stupid—had a stroke or something. Hand doesn't work, words get stuck, leg's got a mind of its own.' He sighed. 'Old age, I suppose. Just because I've retired now it's all going to fall apart.'

His speech was slurred, she thought, and in a curious way he sounded almost like Woody. It gave her the courage to talk to him. She took his hand in hers, the floppy hand that didn't work, and smoothed the skin absently.

'So when did this happen?' she asked.

He shrugged, and it was her mother who answered.

'Tuesday. I would have phoned but you don't have a phone, of course.' There was a note of accusation in her voice but Judith forced herself to ignore it.

'I can't afford a phone.'

'They don't cost much.'

'No, but food is more important.'

Her mother blinked, as if the thought of having to do without food to pay a bill was utterly incomprehensible. Then a soft wash of colour ran up her cheeks. 'Is it really so hard?' she asked quietly.

'It can be. We manage. Just at the moment it's not too bad because I've got a job and the man I'm working for is very generous. In fact, he brought us here today.'

Her mother looked round. 'Us? Is your son here?'

Judith chewed her lip. 'Yes, but he's gone off with Hugh and Alice to find a playground.'

'Isn't he a little old for a playground?' her mother asked in astonishment. 'Oh, of course, he's—er. . .'

Judith helped her out. 'Not for him—for Alice. She's seven.'

'Oh. So where's Hugh's wife while all this is going on?'

Judith could feel the maternal radar switch on. 'She's dead,' she told her mother quietly. 'She died seven years ago when Alice was born.'

'Oh, how frightful. Poor man. Poor child.' There was genuine compassion in her mother's eyes and Judith wondered what it would take to have that compassion aimed in her direction. A little of it would have gone a long way fourteen years ago.

She turned back to her father. 'So, Pop, when are you getting out of here?'

'When the physio's happy I can walk. Have to use a damn fool zimmer thing. Hate it. Look like a grandfather.'

Judith chuckled. 'Dad, you are a grandfather. You've been a grandfather for fourteen years.'

His brow creased. 'Ought to meet the boy really. What's his name again?'

She swallowed. 'Woody.'

'Damn fool name for a boy.'

'It's short for Edward,' she told him, and watched as realisation dawned on him.

'You called him after me,' he quavered. 'Even after we threw you out. . .' Fat tears splashed down his cheeks and onto the crisp white sheet. 'Never should have let it go so far. It was that musician fellow. Waste of space.'

'He was,' Judith agreed. 'But by the time I found out it was too late.'

Her father groped for her hand and crushed it in a desperate grip. 'Don't go again, Jude. Not now. Missed so much. . .'

She hugged him. 'I won't go. I promise. And you ought to meet your grandson.'

He nodded. 'Can he talk? I mean, how bad—? You know. . .' he asked, at last acknowledging the fact that Woody was disabled.

'Oh, yes, he can talk. He can be a little difficult to understand sometimes, but he's all there—his mind isn't affected. He plays a killer game of chess, by the way, and he wants to be a research chemist. You've got a lot in common.'

He blinked. 'Well, fancy that. A chess player.' He looked towards the door. 'Don't suppose you could bring him in to see me?'

Judith thought. Hugh had the mobile phone with him; all it would take was one call, but was Woody ready for it?

'I could try and contact them, but I might not be able to. I'll go and find a phone.'

'Here.' Her mother fished a neat little mobile phone out of her bag and handed it to her, thus depriving her of the opportunity of canvassing Woody for his opinion in private.

Oh, well. She'd have to do it in public. She dialled the number, waited for a moment and then heard Hugh's voice.

'It's Judith. My father would like to meet Woody—I just wondered if you could bring him over if he wants to see them.'

'Hang on, I'll let you talk to him, he's just here. Woody? Your mother.'

She waited a second and then Woody's voice came on the phone.

'Mum? What's wrong?'

'Nothing. Your grandfather would like to meet you if you feel you'd like to see him, but if you don't want to it's all right.'

Her mother bristled but she ignored her. This was

Woody's decision, and no one—most especially not her mother—was going to influence it.

'Now?' he said, after an age.

'If you want to.'

There was another long silence, then, 'Yeah. I would.'

She smiled, not realising until then how much she wanted him to come. 'Thanks. Can I speak to Hugh?'

She asked how long it would take them to get there, and was surprised to find they were only a few minutes away. 'I rather had a feeling this would happen,' Hugh confessed, and she felt a huge surge of love and gratitude for his understanding.

'I'll meet you by the entrance,' she told him. Handing her mother back the phone, she went down to the door and waited.

They weren't long. Hugh arrived with the children in tow, and asked if he should wait with Alice in the car.

'No,' Woody said at once. 'Come too, please.'

Judith sensed his insecurity and his need to have others there to disperse the attention a little. She looked at Hugh, also reassured by his presence. 'Do you mind coming?'

'Of course not.'

So they went back to the ward, and to Judith's astonishment her mother's eyes filled and glittered and she hugged Woody's skinny shoulders and patted him a little helplessly, clearly moved.

'Look, Edward, he's so like you were as a boy,' she told her husband.

He reached out a hand and took Woody's, shaking it formally despite the sparkle of tears in his eyes. 'Well, m'boy, good to meet you at last. Sorry it took so long.'

Woody smiled, a cracked, lopsided smile which Judith recognised hid his awkwardness, and she sat down on the bed and pulled him down beside her, her arm round his shoulders. 'Better late than never. Dad, Mum, this is Hugh

Barber, a friend of ours and currently my employer, and his daughter Alice.'

'Actually, everybody calls me Toots,' Alice said, scrambling up on the bed and plonking herself down by Edward's feet. 'Are you very sick?'

'Well, yes and no. Something's gone a bit wrong in my head—my arm's not too clever and my words all run into each other and I can't walk properly—'

'That sounds just like Woody! So you're not really sick, then, just a bit different. That's OK. Can I have a grape, please?'

Thank God for little children, Judith thought as Alice not only broke the ice but melted it clean away with her bright and chirpy chatter. The rest of the visit was painless, with Hugh chatting to Judith's mother and skilfully avoiding answering her penetrating questions. Woody settled down to a long and technical discussion with his grandfather about computers and industrial chemistry and career opportunities, while all Judith had to do was stop Alice making herself sick with the grapes and watch them all interact.

Then, finally, a nurse came and chivvied them all away.

'Do come again,' her father pleaded, clearly worried they would lose touch once more.

'Of course I will,' she promised. 'Anyway, I expect you'll be home soon.'

He gave a little snort. 'Doubt it. They need torture victims for the physiotherapist,' he said morosely.

'Mum does my physio every night,' Woody told him. 'It's not so bad.'

'Every night?' They looked surprised, her mother's eyes registering what—if Judith didn't know better—she would have thought was admiration.

'It's no big deal,' Woody said with a shrug. 'You get used to it.'

'I'm sure,' his grandmother said a little blankly. 'Judith, thank you for coming.'

Judith smiled. 'My pleasure,' she said, and she knew it was true. It had been a pleasure to see them again. She felt better than she had for ages—for fourteen years, to be precise.

And it was ironic that she should have seen them now when, in a way, history was repeating itself for her.

She wasn't sure yet, of course, but a nagging suspicion was forming at the back of her mind. Her last period had been uncharacteristically light, almost non-existent, and the next one had been missing altogether.

It seemed likely that her parents were going to be grandparents all over again. Perhaps this time, she thought hopefully, it will all turn out all right in the end. . .

Her father continued to improve slowly, and with Hugh's help she and Woody visited him again in hospital. While Woody and her father engaged in earnest conversation, Judith and her mother were thrown together and they cautiously became friends again.

It wasn't easy for either of them, but gradually they began to bridge the yawning chasm between them. Judith told her about bringing Woody up, and what they had been doing along the way, and her mother talked about her job at the museum and her father's job at a research station—and slowly the thaw set in.

And, of course, they talked about Edward senior and his slow recovery.

'I don't know what he's going to be like by Christmas,' her mother said in the middle of December. 'We'd booked a mini-cruise off the Florida coast, but he won't be well enough to fly out there, I shouldn't think.'

A mini-cruise in Florida? Judith thought, and tried not to imagine how much it must have cost. They were both successful professionals and there was no reason why they shouldn't spend their money on themselves. It was just that she could see Christmas as a minefield of expense that she could ill afford. There wasn't only Woody to consider now, of course. She had to buy presents for Martin and Alice, as well as Hugh—

'What do you think about him flying out there?' her mother asked, still worrying about the cruise.

'I should ask the doctors. Personally I think he'd find it too tiring.'

'Hmm. I wondered. I just didn't want to cancel because he's been looking forward to it so much. We'd planned it as a retirement treat—I know he retired in August but the weather here is always so dismal in December.' She looked at Judith a little warily. 'What are your plans for Christmas?'

Judith was suddenly very glad she had some. The thought of spending Christmas with her parents was too much too soon, and she had a strange feeling that was going to be the next question.

'Actually, Hugh asked us if we'd join them.'

'That's nice.' Her mother's eyes were searching and missed nothing. 'You're in love with him, aren't you?' Her softly voiced remark wasn't really a question, and Judith didn't intend to answer it as one. She shot a speaking glance at her son's back, and Marion obligingly picked up the cue and dropped the subject. Good. Judith wasn't ready to discuss their relationship with her mother.

'Edward's coming home next week,' the older woman said. 'I'll make a decision then about the cruise. Perhaps we'll postpone it to the spring and just have a quiet day at home on our own—unless you want to change your plans and join us?'

She sounded a little wistful and for a second Judith felt almost torn, but this Christmas was to be a sort of test for them all and she badly needed it to go well. 'I'm sorry, I can't,' she said softly. 'It's our first Christmas, and we're all looking forward to it.' All except Martin, she thought worriedly. 'Perhaps we can come over for New Year or something?'

'That would be lovely—anyway, if you change your mind we'll be there and you're most welcome—I can't see us going on the cruise, really.'

'No,' Judith agreed. Oh, dear, she sounded so mournful. Did she really want them there for Christmas? And what if it was her father's last? No, she thought, I'm not going to change my plans out of guilt and duty. She still hadn't told Hugh about the baby, and she was hoping that if things worked out it would be easier to tell him. Whatever happened he had to know soon, but Martin's reaction would be the key. She owed it to all the children, born and unborn, to make sure they had a future together.

She was glad when Hugh collected them a short while later. It was good to be back in touch with her parents again but she had her own life now, and it was with Hugh. Hugh and his children. Oh, please, God, let it be all right, she thought desperately.

The week before Christmas was bedlam, of course. Because Hugh was closing the surgery at midday on Christmas Eve—and not reopening until the Monday after Christmas—patients were panic-striken. The upholsterer with the recurrent low back strain had lifted another sofa and prostrated himself for a few days, and Hugh was working hard to keep him mobile so he could meet his Christmas deadline.

'Why do they all want the stuff for Christmas and think of it at the end of November?' he grumbled good-naturedly to Judith at ten o'clock on Christmas Eve. 'I could be dead before I finish this suite, and all so some snotty-nosed little kid can crush chocolates into it on Christmas afternoon. They must be mad, all of them.'

He grinned, wished her a merry Christmas and limped

out of the door to go back to his deadline. How he would finish off the furniture and deliver it in time she had no idea, but she was certain it wouldn't improve his Christmas one iota.

She wondered when and if he had found time to do any Christmas shopping. Perhaps his wife did it? Judith had gone to town last Saturday and bought all her presents, and they were wrapped and sitting in her wardrobe at home waiting for Hugh to pick them up and bring them round later today.

He was going to do the food shopping later, and she was going to help the children decorate the tree. It was up in the snug, a huge tree that filled one corner completely, and Hugh had already strung the lights and checked that they worked. All she and the children had to do was decorate it with the baubles and tinsel and it would be done.

It sounded so easy. The first hurdle they had to overcome, however, was the ornaments.

'What are these?' Martin asked, looking shocked.

'Oh, they're pretty! Let me see!' Alice snatched the Victorian-style bauble and studied it intently. 'Oh, I love it! Look, Marty, it's got carol singers all over it—'

'It's gross. Where are the old ones?'

Judith sat back on her heels and sighed softly to herself. Here we go, she thought. 'I don't know. Your father left these out and asked us to put them up.'

'They're the wrong ones,' Martin said mutinously.

'Maybe he thought the other ones were old and worn out,' Woody suggested hesitantly.

Martin shot him a fulminating glare. 'Keep out of this, Spaz. It's not your business.'

'Martin,' Judith began warningly, but he threw a bauble across the room and glared at her, too.

'What? It isn't his business. Come to that, it isn't yours, either. It isn't your house, it isn't your tree and it isn't up to you how we decorate it! I'm going to find the other ones.'

He ran out, leaving Judith, Woody and Alice sitting in shocked silence. Moments later he was back again, his arms full of dusty boxes dragged from the attic, and he started hanging the old, worn baubles with grim determination.

'Well, come on, then, Alice, help me,' he ordered.

'No. I liked the new ones,' she said mutinously, and her lip wobbled.

'How about putting up a selection of both?' Judith suggested, trying to be diplomatic, but she might as well have saved her breath.

'It wouldn't be the same,' Martin said, almost throwing the ornaments onto the tree.

'Does it have to be?' she asked quietly.

'Yes!' He turned on her, his eyes filled with rage and helplessness and despair. 'Since you've been around nothing's been the same! Dad doesn't have time for us any more. He's either shut up in the office with you, doing God knows what, or playing chess with your son. He never does anything with us any more, and the way he looks at you's disgusting.

'I know what you get up to—I've been counting the condoms in the bedside chest. You do it every lunchtime, don't you? Sneak upstairs while there's nobody around—'

'Do what?'

'Never mind, Toots,' Martin and Judith both said at once, and Alice looked at Woody.

'Do what?' she asked again. 'Why are they fighting?'

'Hush, Toots,' Woody murmured and held out his arms to her.

She scooted into them, and Martin turned his attention back to Woody. 'That's right, suck up to the kid. You make me sick.'

'You're upsetting her—'

'Shame—and you don't think you're upsetting me?' He turned back to Judith. 'As for you, creeping round Dad just so you can live in a nice house and get free food and free treatment and free—'

'Martin, I think that's quite enough,' Judith interrupted firmly, unable to sit back and let him run on any longer. It didn't stop him, though. If anything, it made him worse.

'Oh, do you think it's quite enough?' he sneered. 'Well, isn't it a pity about you? You're not my mother, you aren't ever going to be my mother or Alice's mother, and you can just stop acting as if you are and leave us all alone. We don't want you here! Christmas is for families, and you aren't our family and you aren't ever going to be so I don't know why you're going to be here at all! Why don't you just get out?'

Judith said nothing. Her eyes filling with tears, she set the box of ornaments down, stood up and brushed off her skirt absently.

'Perhaps you're right,' she said, and her voice sounded rusty and unused. 'Woody, come on.'

'And you can take your presents with you,' Martin yelled, throwing the parcels across the room. One crashed into the wall with the sound of breaking glass, and for a second there was a shocked silence.

Then Martin barged past them and ran sobbing up the stairs, leaving Judith shaking in the middle of the room. She felt Woody's arm round her shoulders and straightened them with a huge effort. Then she walked out of the room, sat down at the beautiful desk in the hall and with a trembling hand she wrote, 'We won't be here for Christmas after all. Sorry to mess you about. Will talk later. Love, Judith'.

She left it on the desk where he was bound to see it when he returned, and brushed the wet blobs off it where her tears had fallen. 'Come on,' Woody said gently, and helped her into her coat.

Alice was sobbing hysterically, clawing at Judith and Woody, but Judith just had to get out, to get away, to escape.

'Sorry, Toots,' she whispered brokenly, and with one last hug she prised the little hands off and almost ran out of the door.

All the way home Woody struggled to keep up with her, but she had to get through her own front door before she could collapse and there wasn't time to go slowly. . .

She dashed the tears from her cheeks and kept walking, and somehow Woody stayed with her—all the way up the path and into her bedroom. Then she threw herself down on the bed, buried her head under the pillow and sobbed her heart out.

When she finally slowed to a hiccupping halt Woody patted her shoulder awkwardly. 'How about a cup of tea?' he suggested, and she knelt up in the middle of the bed and blew her nose and tried to suppress the last few sobs.

'Thanks,' she managed eventually. 'That would be lovely.'

He went reluctantly out of the room, looking over his shoulder as he went, and his face was wet and blotched and concerned.

Oh, Hugh, she thought, where do we go from here? You, me and our baby?

Fat tears spilled down her cheeks again and she brushed them aside angrily. No. She wouldn't cry any more. She'd done this once, she could do it again—but this time she'd have the help of her parents. They needed to be involved and they wanted to be involved, she knew. This time would be different.

She found Woody in the kitchen, sniffing over the teapot, and she turned him into her arms and hugged him hard.

'I love you,' she told him fiercely.

'I know. I love you too, Mum,' he said, hugging her back.

'After we've had a cup of tea,' she told him, 'we're going to pack some things, get on the train and go and stay with my parents for Christmas. They're just spending it quietly at home, and I know we'll be welcome there.'

Woody nodded, and while she packed he made the tea and they sat in her bedroom surrounded by cases and presents. Judith had to sort out the ones for Hugh and Martin and Alice and put them on one side. What would become of them she didn't know, but she couldn't think about that now. She had to focus on today, this minute, right now. The future, frankly, didn't bear consideration.

CHAPTER ELEVEN

'MARTIN?'

Hugh looked around the snug, strewn with baubles and presents and tinsel flung every which way, and Alice wrapped her little arms round his hips and buried her head in his coat and sobbed as if her heart was breaking.

'Martin?' he yelled again. 'Judith?'

'Gone,' Toots hiccuped.

Hugh felt a chill of fear run down his spine. Gone? How could she be gone? He crouched down and took Alice's shaking shoulders in his hands. 'Toots? Talk to me, sweetheart. Where's Judith gone? What's happened?'

Surely they hadn't all gone out and left Alice alone?

'Marty told her to go away,' Toots hiccuped, 'so she did. He broke my picture—'

Hugh looked round and saw the broken edge of a picture frame sticking out of a crumpled wrapper. There was a big gouge in the wall above, as if the picture had been hurled with considerable force, and he could only wonder at the scene that had taken place.

'Where's Martin?' he asked Alice, straightening up, his mouth a grim line.

'Upstairs. He's crying.'

Hugh dragged a hand over his face and patted Toots on the head. 'Come in the kitchen and let me wash your face and find you a biscuit, then I'm going to have a chat to Martin and see if I can find out what's going on.'

'They had a row,' Toots volunteered. 'About the ornaments. Marty wanted the old ones again and he wouldn't have the new ones, and he said everything had changed— Daddy, what's a condom?'

Hugh stopped in his tracks and Alice turned and looked up at him, innocently questioning.

'Um—never mind now.' Where the hell had that come from? he wondered. 'Tell me about the row.'

'He said he'd been counting them and you did it every day and you never did things with us but it isn't true. It's just that he doesn't like Punch and Judy, but I love them and now he's sent them away. . .'

Alice started to cry again and Hugh scooped her up and hugged her, carrying her through to the kitchen and sitting her on the worktop while he washed her face. 'Here, have a biscuit.'

The hiccuping sobs stopped. 'Can I have a chocolate one?'

Hugh had bought a tin of them for Christmas, but he had a horrible, sinking feeling they wouldn't be needed. Damn Martin. He opened the tin, let Alice choose two and then put the lid on again.

'Right,' he said with more calm than he felt. 'I'm going up to talk to Martin, and you're going to put these things away for me in the fridge. OK, Toots?'

She nodded, munching her biscuit, and he lifted her down, ruffled her hair and went upstairs three at a time to the attic.

He found Martin face down in the middle of his bed, his shoulders still shaking with sobs.

'Go away,' he howled, flinging his father's hand away.

'No. Martin, we have to talk. Come on, I want to know what's going on.'

'I'm sure Toots has told you,' he said bitterly.

'I want to hear it from you.'

'No, you don't,' Martin mumbled, his voice clogged with tears. 'You won't want to talk to me at all when you know what I've done.'

With a ragged sigh Hugh sat down with his back against the headboard and pulled his son across his chest. 'Rubbish. I love you, Martin. Whatever the problem is we can sort it out. Now talk to me. Tell me what went wrong.'

Martin sniffed and scrubbed his nose against Hugh's shirt. 'It was the ornaments. We always have the others. We used to put them up with Mum—'

He broke off, and Hugh stroked his hair and hugged him. 'Just that?' he said softly. 'It was really just the ornaments?'

Martin shook his head. 'No. It was everything. She's always here—you do things—oh, God, Dad, she's not my mum, she doesn't belong here—'

'Just because she's not your mother? Don't you think there could be room for her as my wife?'

Martin struggled out of his Hugh's arms and sat up in the middle of the bed, hugging his knees to his chest. 'No! You spend all your time with her now, anyway. I just feel I'm losing you as well as Mum. . .'

With a ragged groan Hugh put his arms round Martin, cradling him against his chest. 'No, Marty, you're not losing me. You'll never lose me, not as long as there's still breath in my body. Sorry, mate, you're stuck with me, like it or not. You're not losing me at all. You're gaining Judith and Woody—or is that the problem?'

'Woody? No, he's OK. I pick on him but it's just to get at her. . .'

He sobbed again, and Hugh stroked his shoulders and let him cry for a moment.

'So you and Woody don't really get on that badly? You could learn to live with each other?'

'Yeah—but it's not him, it's Judith. I just feel you don't care about us any more—all you can think about is her.' He ducked his head a little and then went on, 'I know what you do. I've been checking the condoms in your bedside chest.'

So that's where the comment from Toots came from,

Hugh thought with a sigh. Lord, the gloves had really been off downstairs.

'Look, I know you find this difficult but I'm lonely, Marty. I'm still young, really. I was only twenty-eight when your mother died. I still remember her with a great deal of love, but she's not here any more and I am—and so is Judith. Is it so very wrong that we've found happiness together?'

'Don't you mean sex?'

He sighed again. 'No, Martin, I don't mean sex. I mean happiness. I haven't felt like this since your mother was alive and, to be honest, it feels wonderful. I feel whole again, as if it's all worth fighting for.' He hesitated, unsure how to continue, then went on, 'I love her, Marty. She's kind and generous and funny and clever, and she takes so little for granted. She's had a hell of a life but she never asks for anything for herself, only for Edward.'

Martin took a great shaky breath. 'I accused her of freeloading,' he confessed miserably. 'I told her she wasn't family and we didn't want her, and now we're going to have a horrible Christmas and it's all my fault. . .'

He crumpled again, sagging against Hugh and sobbing miserably. Hugh didn't know whether to hug him or strangle him. God alone knows what Judith's feeling, he thought.

'Martin, I have to go and find her. Go downstairs and tidy up the snug and put the rest of the decorations on the tree, then help Toots put the shopping away. I'll be back soon.'

'With Judith?'

'Do you want her back?'

He nodded miserably. 'It's not that I don't like her—I do. It's just I felt I was losing you, and I can't go through it again—'

Hugh crushed him against his chest and pressed a kiss to his damp and tangled hair. 'It's all right, Marty,' he said gruffly. 'I'll sort it out and bring her back. Don't cry any more, come on.'

'Which decorations?' Martin asked in a small voice.

'I don't care so long as the tree looks pretty. Use them all, if you like.'

Martin nodded, and they went downstairs together. Hugh jumped in the car and drove round to Judith's flat. All he had to do now was convince her to come home with him and everything would be all right—but that was going to be no mean achievement.

There were no lights on when he pulled up outside. He ran up the path and rang the bell, then pounded on the door and tried to peer through the window but it was too high up. He went back to the letterbox and yelled her name through it, but the flat was in silence.

He had no choice but to give up. He scribbled a note and poked it through the flap. It was possible they were inside in the dark, but he doubted it.

Just for good measure, though, he yelled once again.

'No good doing that—they've gone away for Christmas. Taxi came for them about half an hour ago.'

Hugh straightened up and turned round, and found a homely woman leaning on the fence. 'Any idea where?' he asked her.

'No—and if I did I shouldn't tell you. She'd been crying—Woody, too.'

Hugh swore softly under his breath. 'Look, if she should come back tell her I was here, could you? Hugh. Ask her to call me.' He hesitated, then added, 'Tell her I love her.'

The woman searched his face for a moment, then seemed to relent. 'Might have gone to her folks. Said a week ago her mum had asked her, but she was coming to you. Might have changed her mind.' She settled herself more comfortably on the fence. 'Had a row, did you?'

Hugh forced himself to be polite. He was her only link

with Judith at the moment, and he didn't want to offend her. 'Sort of. My son upset her. Look, I have to go. If she turns up, if you wouldn't mind giving her the message?'

The woman nodded and watched impassively as he ran down the path and got back in the car. He had to force himself to remember the speed limit as he drove off, conscious of the woman's curious and disapproving stare.

He went home and helped with the clean-up operation, rescued the painting Toots had done for Judith and managed to find another frame to put it in, soothed Martin's ragged nerves—and all the time he willed the phone to ring.

Refusing to wait any longer, grabbing the phone book, he thumbed through the Ws until he found a listing for Wright, Edward. That had to be him—it was the only one in the Ipswich area. Rushmere Road. He memorised the address—just in case—and picked up the phone.

It was definitely theirs. He recognised Mrs Wright's voice on the recorded message. Lord, how he hated answerphones. What could he say to one today that wouldn't sound unbelieveably crass and stupid?

So he said nothing the first three times he rang, and then finally he spoke. 'This is Hugh Barber. Judith, if you're there, please call me. I've spoken to Martin and it's all right. Please ring me. Please come back.' He paused for a second. 'I love you,' he added softly, then cradled the phone and rested his head against the wall.

'Oh, God, Judith, ring me,' he whispered, his voice clogged with tears.

'Dad?'

He took a steadying breath and squared his shoulders. 'Yes?'

'I'm sorry.'

He turned round and held out his arms, and Martin fell into them, clinging to him and sobbing. 'It's going to be the worst Christmas of my life, and it's all my fault. I've ruined it for everybody,' he wept.

Hugh patted him helplessly and struggled against the tears that were threatening to engulf him. He had to keep calm. It was only a matter of time before she rang him back. She would ring, he knew it.

Wouldn't she. . .?

Judith stared at the answerphone in silence. Her head was pounding, her eyes burned and her throat ached from holding back tears. Did she dare believe him? Was Martin really all right? She couldn't believe he was, not after the things he'd said. He hated her, that much was clear. There was no way Hugh could have changed that. Her hand slid down until it lay protectively over their child. What would become of it if they couldn't work things out?

She'd cope, of course, but she'd had such dreams, such plans—

'You love him very much, don't you?' her mother said.

She yanked in a shaking breath. 'Yes. Yes, I do.'

'You have to talk to him.'

'Why? So he can talk me into going back and we can make Martin's life a misery? He hates me, Mum.'

'No. He's just a mixed-up kid. He probably hates himself more than anybody else at the moment.'

Just then the phone rang again. Judith's eyes locked on it and as her mother's message finished she heard ragged breathing for a second, then Martin's voice. 'Judith? I'm sorry. Please come back.'

She hesitated for a second, then snatched up the phone. 'Martin?'

'Judith? I'm sorry—'

'Martin, it's OK. I understand. Let me speak to your father, please. I need to talk to him.'

'Um—I don't know where he is. I'll get him. Hang on.'

She heard him calling, then seconds later Hugh's voice

came over the line, shaking with emotion. 'Judith? Are you all right?'

She closed her eyes, so relieved to hear his voice that she couldn't speak.

'Judith? Judith, are you there? Speak to me!'

'I'm here. Did you get my note?'

'No. What note?'

'On the desk in the hall.'

'No. Forget the note. I'm coming to get you.'

'No. Hugh, please. Give me some time. Give Martin time, too. He hates me—'

'No. He loves me. He didn't think I could love both you and him at the same time, that's all. The Christmas decorations were just an impulse buy, but he thought it was all part of cutting off our old life because you were around. It was a stupid move. I just didn't think about how he'd feel—he used to decorate the tree with Linda.' He hesitated a second, then went on, 'Judith, please, come back. We need you.'

She chewed her lip, still torn. 'I've said I'll stay here now. My father's really delighted and he'll be so disappointed if I take Woody away from him.'

'They could come, too,' he said instantly.

'Hugh, you don't want us all—'

'I do. I want you more than I can ever express, and if that means your entire family or even the whole of Suffolk, so be it.'

She turned and looked at her mother. 'I'll have to ask them. I'll call you back.'

'Do it quickly. I love you.'

She hung up. She couldn't say the words, not in front of her mother and with her emotions running so close to the surface.

'He wants you and Dad to come as well,' she said without expression.

'Do you want to go?'

She tried to sound dispassionate but it was impossible. 'Yes,' she said tearfully. 'Yes, I want to go to him. To them. And I want you to come—if you will.'

'Then you'd better call him back, hadn't you, and tell him we'll be there at eight in the morning?'

A huge smile broke out on Judith's face. 'Thanks, Mum,' she cried, and then she was in her mother's arms, having the first hug she'd had from her in years, and it felt so good she didn't ever want to let go.

She did, though, but only long enough to ring Hugh and tell him they'd be coming.

'Thank God,' he said fervently. 'Tell your mother to drive carefully.'

'Will do. I love you.'

He gave a gusty sigh. 'I love you, too, darling. I'm sorry.'

'Don't be. It wasn't your fault.'

'It was. I should have seen what was happening with Martin.'

'You're not a mind-reader, Hugh, you're just a father. Stop trying to be perfect and just tell him you love him, and we'll see you in the morning.'

She put the phone down and turned back to her mother. 'He said drive carefully.'

Her mother smiled. 'Of course. I've got my grand-children to consider, haven't I?'

Judith's smile faltered. 'Grandchildren?' she whispered.

'Yes. Does he know yet, by the way?'

She shook her head, speechless. 'No. No, he doesn't.'

'It'll make a nice Christmas present, then, won't it? Talking of which, I think I've got a case of rather nice wine out the back—do you suppose he'd like it for Christmas?'

*   *   *

It was a fairly subdued party that travelled up from Ipswich the following morning. Judith, dreading her meeting with Martin, chewed her lip until it was almost raw, her hands clenched in her lap. Beside her Woody was unnaturally quiet, even for him, darting her anxious glances every now and again.

She wondered how he really felt and if going to Hugh's for Christmas, instead of spending it quietly with the grandfather he clearly idolised, was actually what he wanted to do.

That grandfather was dozing, still finding everything very tiring after his stroke, and behind the wheel of the car her mother concentrated on the road and said nothing, busy with her own thoughts.

She'd dropped everything—not that there'd been much to drop as she hadn't been expecting visitors, but she'd put her preparations aside and fallen in with Hugh's request without a murmur of protest.

Now, as they arrived, Judith's palms were tingling and damp with dread, her mouth was dry and she thought her breath was going to jam in her throat. Before Marion had even turned off the engine, however, Judith's door was snatched open and she was hauled unceremoniously out of the car into Hugh's arms.

There was no reserve, no hesitation, just a desperate man finally reunited with his love after one of the longest nights of his life.

It felt wonderful. She wrapped her arms round him, turned her face up for his kiss and didn't care who saw her.

After a second he lifted his head and smoothed her hair back. 'It's so good to see you,' he said fervently. 'You can have no idea.'

'Oh, I think I can,' she replied, her voice trembling. 'How's Martin?'

'Worried to death that you won't forgive him. He

wouldn't come out. He's in the hall.'

'I'll go and see him.' She eased herself out of Hugh's arms and went inside, leaving the others in Hugh's charge. She didn't know what she was going to say. She just hoped she could find the right words to heal the gulf between them, because otherwise the future was too bleak to bear thinking about.

'Martin?' she called. 'Are you here?'

He was just round the corner, sitting on the bottom stair. She sat beside him, squeezing into the gap. He shifted up a little to make room for her—or was it to move away?

'Hi,' she said softly.

He didn't say a thing. He just turned towards her, buried his face in her bosom and sobbed his heart out. She hugged him, rocking him gently, and thought how awful it was to be so young and vulnerable to other people's wishes and manoeuvrings.

After a while she gave him a little squeeze. 'Hey, lighten up, young man, it's supposed to be Christmas.'

'I've ruined it,' he sniffed wretchedly.

'No, you haven't. It's only just beginning. We could always call a truce.'

He sniffed again and scrubbed his nose on his sleeve. 'I thought you'd take Dad away from me,' he said, tears threatening again.

'Oh, Marty, don't be silly,' she said warmly, hugging him hard. 'I want to be with all of you. I was hoping we could become one big family. Maybe I was just being naïve, but I really imagined that you and Woody might learn to get on, and I could be the mother little Alice has never had, and that your father and I could be happy together.'

'It sounds really nice,' Martin said wistfully, so quietly she could hardly hear him.

'Well, it's not too late. Shall we go for it?'

He looked up and grinned ruefully. 'Can we?'

She wrinkled her nose. 'Yeah. Now, you go and wash your hands and splash your face and come and join us all—OK?

She watched him walk down the hall to the cloakroom, and then went into the snug. The tree looked gaudy and overdressed—and wonderful. So did Hugh, who was instantly by her side. 'OK?'

She smiled up at him, her heart in her eyes. 'Yes. Yes, it's OK.'

'Thank God for that.' His smile warmed her as nothing else could have done. 'Is he coming?'

'He's washing his face.'

The door opened and Martin slipped in behind them, still a little red-eyed but more composed. Hugh hugged him to his side, and then turned to everyone.

'I think it's time to open the presents, don't you?'

Judith wondered if everyone might be a little polite and formal, but Toots dispatched that at a stroke. 'Yippee,' she said and, plonking herself down in front of the tree, she started dishing out presents.

'That's Daddy's—and this one's for Woody, and this is for me—wonder what it is?' she said, shaking it and putting it to one side. 'Here's Judith's—it got broken,' she explained, shooting Martin a speaking look, 'but Daddy fixed it, sort of. It's from me.'

'Right. Thank you.' Judith took the present, a flat parcel the side of a large magazine but quite rigid, and carefully removed the wrapping paper. It was a painting, one of the sort Alice did at school, and it depicted a man and a woman and three children—two boys and a younger girl. At least, that was what Judith thought they were meant to be. Anyway, they were all smiling huge curly smiles, and it was obviously a happy scene.

And, if she looked closely, there was a tear in one

corner and a little cut across the centre, carefully patched and repaired.

'It's meant to be us,' Alice explained, holding her breath. 'I thought if I painted us it might come true, but then Marty smashed it.'

Judith felt her eyes fill. 'Oh, Toots,' she said in a shaky little voice. 'It's lovely, darling, and it's not damaged, not really. Perhaps the little cut will help us all remember not to take each other for granted.'

She looked across at Martin who looked wretched again. 'Won't it?' she said gently.

He nodded. 'I haven't got you a present,' he confessed miserably.

'Yes, you have,' she told him. 'You've given me the best present in the world—you've let me and Woody come into your family. What more could I possibly want?'

Martin blushed scarlet and mumbled something unintelligible, her parents exchanged a relieved smile, Woody swallowed hard and across the room Hugh's eyes sparkled a brilliant blue. His throat worked furiously for a second, and then he grinned.

'OK, guys, that's enough soppy stuff. I'm sure there's something for Woody in there, and Martin.'

He pulled out two identical packages and handed them to the boys, who opened them and then blushed simultaneously.

'Electric razors?' Edward senior said with a chuckle. 'When I started shaving I had to cut myself, just like anybody else. I remember. . .'

He rambled gently on while Hugh dished out the presents and Judith helped Alice with a particularly stubborn bit of sticky tape. Finally the room looked like a colourful paper-chase and all the presents were unwrapped.

Well, almost all. There was nothing for Judith from Hugh, and Toots hadn't failed to notice the omission.

'There must be one here,' she said, her arms flailing as she swiped the wrapping paper out of the way of her search.

'I've got it in my pocket,' Hugh told her.

'But why? It should be under the tree.'

He shook his head. 'Not this present. I want to give it to Judith on her own.'

He held his hand out to her and pulled her to her feet. 'Come on. I need to check the turkey, anyway.'

They went into the kitchen, and with a huge sigh Hugh pulled her into his arms and hugged her. 'Well done. I thought you handled that brilliantly,' he mumbled into her hair. 'I love you so much—have I mentioned that?'

She laughed breathlessly. 'Just once or twice, but I won't get sick of hearing it, I promise you.'

'Good, because I intend to say it rather a lot.'

He released her and slipped his hand into his trouser pocket, pulling out a jeweller's box. He flipped the lid, lifted out a ring and slid it onto her finger. A simple gold band with five beautiful diamonds in a rubbed-over Victorian setting, it fitted perfectly. 'There,' he said with satisfaction, 'now you really are mine.' And he kissed her lingeringly, and very thoroughly.

Fortunately the turkey was fine because it was some considerable time before either of them had the presence of mind to bother to check it. . .

The kitchen was in chaos, but it was quiet compared to the rowdy scene in the snug and only a little untidier than the waiting room which they had turned back into a dining room for their Christmas lunch. There were paper hats and streamers all over the floor, the plates and glasses were still strewn all over the table, and the party had decamped to the snug for an afternoon of television and seeing who could eat the most chocolates without being sick.

In the relative sanctuary of the kitchen Hugh put his arms round Judith and lowered his mouth to hers. 'Mmm. You taste of chocolate mint crisps,' he murmured against her lips. 'Delicious. . .'

'Hugh?'

'Hmm?' he mumbled.

She put her hands on his shoulders and eased him away. 'I've got something to tell you,' she said, looking up into his smouldering blue eyes.

Raising his head at last he looked down at her and searched her face. 'Good or bad?' he asked carefully.

She smiled nervously. 'That rather depends on your perspective.'

'Fire away, then. The suspense is killing me.'

She studied his Adam's apple for a moment. Funny, she'd never really noticed it before. . .

'Judith?'

Her eyes flicked back up to his. 'Um—I'm—we're—that is. . .'

'Spit it out, darling.' His voice was laced with indulgent laughter.

'I'm pregnant,' she said in a rush.

He went absolutely still, then something quite incredible happened in the back of his eyes. 'Oh, Judith,' he breathed. 'Oh, darling—when? How?'

She chuckled, infinitely relieved by his response. 'The first time, I suppose—and the usual way.'

He looked at her for what seemed an age, then his arms wrapped her hard against his chest and his mouth found hers and he was kissing her as if she was the most precious thing he'd ever held.

'Here they are—oh, yuck.'

They drew slowly apart and turned to look at their audience: Martin and Woody, looking teenaged and faintly embarrassed; Toots looking frankly curious;

Marion looking satisfied, and Edward Senior positively bursting with delight.

'Celebrating something?' Marion asked mildly.

'Actually, yes,' Hugh said with a grin. 'We're going to have a baby.'

'Wow, great—but I thought you were using—' Martin began, and then yelped when Woody kicked him. The Wrights looked much as before but more so. Only Toots looked appalled. To Judith's consternation she started to cry, great huge tears rolling down her cheeks.

'Toots—what is it, sweetheart? Wouldn't you like a baby sister or brother?' Hugh asked, gathering the weeping child into his arms.

'I don't want her to die,' she sobbed.

Judith closed her eyes and almost laughed with relief. 'Toots, I'm not going to die, darling. Your mummy was sick—that was why she died. I'm not sick. I'll be fine. You'll see. Everything will be all right.'

'Promise?' she asked tearfully.

Judith swallowed. 'I can't promise,' she said earnestly, 'because it's not in my power to control it, but I'm as sure as I can be that everything will be all right.'

Alice looked from her to Hugh and back again. 'Good,' she said, 'because I love you and I don't want you to go again.'

Judith smiled and hugged the little girl in her father's arms. 'Don't you worry, Toots. I'm not going anywhere without you—all of you. And that,' she added, '*is* a promise. . .'

EPILOGUE

JUDITH sank into the little sofa in the kitchen with a sigh. The place was in chaos, but at least it was a bit quieter than the snug.

Only a bit. Belinda was jabbering on her knee, chewing her fingers and dribbling. Judith eyed her adoringly. She had brought them all such happiness already in her short life, and she simply couldn't imagine life without the little scamp.

Named not only for Linda, Hugh's first wife and the mother of his children, she was also called after Belle, Al's mother, who had arrived in the nick of time to deliver her after a frantic phone call. She had been in even more of a hurry than Christine's baby, but unlike Judith's first labour this one had been easy.

That was the trouble, of course. She'd hardly even realised she was in labour before Bella had made her appearance. There had been one huge advantage to the easy birth, of course. The trauma Woody had suffered had mercifully passed her by—and although lightning wasn't supposed to strike in the same place twice Judith was still relieved as Bella grew and developed quite normally. In fact, she was being plagued by one of those developmental stages right now.

'You're teething, aren't you?' she said, and the baby turned and grabbed Judith's shoulders and pulled herself up, bouncing on her lap.

'Mum-mum-mum-mum,' she sang in her little cherub's voice.

'Oh, you tub, you're so full of it. Have you had a lovely Christmas Day?'

'I think they all have.' The sofa sank beside her and she turned to see Hugh, a yellow paper hat leaning drunkenly on his head.

'Hi there,' she said with a grin.

'Hi. Do you suppose there's any chance we can sneak upstairs and put that little thing to bed and catch a few quiet minutes?'

She laughed softly. 'In your dreams. Does she look tired?'

He shook his head mournfully. 'No, she looks disgustingly wide awake. The trouble is, by the time she's asleep I will be, too.'

Judith smiled. 'That's families for you.'

'Mmm.' Dropping his head back against the sofa, he sighed luxuriously. He patted the newly revamped cushions, his expression benign, and rolled his head towards her with a lazy smile. 'I'm glad we kept this old thing. It's come in very handy, what with you and Christine both having babies on it, and it's awfully nice to be able to sneak in here and grab a few quiet seconds on something comfy.'

Belinda shrieked, just to punctuate his remark, and he winced and reached for her. 'You, young lady, are too noisy for words. I wonder if your brothers want to look after you?'

'I think you'll find Woody's thrashing my father at chess and Martin's giving my mother a hard time for cheating at Scrabble.'

Hugh chuckled. 'There's always Toots.'

'She's teaching the puppy not to wee on the carpet in the hall.'

'Oh, Lord—stuck with you, are we, Bella?'

He hitched up her little dress and blew a loud raspberry on her chubby tummy, and the baby folded in half with a giggle and smacked his face with her tubby little hands, before snuggling into him and blowing bubbles all over his new shirt.

He looked at Judith over her head and gave a lazy wink. 'Later,' he promised.

She laughed. 'I'll hold you to that.'

'You do that. I'll count on it. I want my Christmas present.'

His smile warmed her, right through to the bottom of her heart. . .

MILLS & BOON®

Medical Romance™

COMING NEXT MONTH

TO HAVE AND TO HOLD by Laura MacDonald

Book 1 Matchmaker Quartet

Georgina and Andrew had been married, now they were divorced. But their friend Helen knew it would only take a little gentle persuasion to get them back together again.

———∿———

THIRD TIME LUCKY by Josie Metcalfe

Final book St Augustine's *trilogy*

Hannah had her own reasons for not wanting a relationship. but when she finally sees Leo as more than a colleague, she finds it impossible *not* to get involved.

———∿———

HEALING THE BREAK by Patricia Robertson

The whole hospital believed Heather and Scott were a hot item. To stop the gossip, they decided to act—they would pretend to date and then end the relationship. Simple—or was it?

———∿———

A SURGEON'S SEARCH by Helen Shelton

Tessa wanted to say yes to James, but she knew she should say no—after all, James was her best friend. He couldn't be serious about wanting more, could he?

WINTER WARMERS

How would you like to win a year's supply of Mills & Boon® books? Well you can and they're FREE! Simply complete the competition below and send it to us by 30th June 1998. The first five correct entries picked after the closing date will each win a year's subscription to the Mills & Boon series of their choice. What could be easier?

THERMAL SOCKS   RAINCOAT   RADIATOR

TIGHTS   WOOLY HAT   CARDIGAN

BLANKET   SCARF   LOG FIRE

WELLINGTONS   GLOVES   JUMPER

T	H	E	R	M	A	L	S	O	C	K	S
I	Q	S	R	E	P	M	U	J	I	N	O
G	A	S	T	I	S	N	O	I	O	E	E
H	T	G	R	A	D	I	A	T	O	R	L
T	A	C	A	R	D	I	G	A	N	A	T
S	H	F	G	O	L	N	Q	S	W	I	E
J	Y	H	J	K	I	Y	R	C	A	N	K
H	L	F	N	L	W	E	T	A	N	C	N
B	O	V	L	O	G	F	I	R	E	O	A
D	O	E	A	D	F	G	J	F	K	A	L
C	W	A	E	G	L	O	V	E	S	T	B

C7L

Please turn over for details of how to enter ⇨

HOW TO ENTER

There is a list of twelve items overleaf all of which are used to keep you warm and dry when it's cold and wet. Each of these items, is hidden somewhere in the grid for you to find. They may appear forwards, backwards or diagonally. As you find each one, draw a line through it. When you have found all twelve, don't forget to fill in the coupon below, pop this page into an envelope and post it today—you don't even need a stamp! Hurry competition ends 30th June 1998.

Mills & Boon Winter Warmers Competition FREEPOST CN81, Croydon, Surrey, CR9 3WZ
EIRE readers send competition to PO Box 4546, Dublin 24.

Please tick the series you would like to receive
if you are one of the lucky winners

Presents™ ❑ Enchanted™ ❑ Medical Romance™ ❑
Historical Romance™ ❑ Temptation® ❑

Are you a Reader Service™ Subscriber? Yes ❑ No ❑

Mrs/Ms/Miss/Mr.........................Initials ....
(BLOCK CAPITALS PLEASE)

Surname ....

Address ....

....

....Postcode ....

(I am over 18 years of age)   C7L

One application per household. Competition open to residents of the UK and Ireland only. You may be mailed with offers from other reputable companies as a result of this application. If you would prefer not to receive such offers, please tick box. ❑

Mills & Boon® is a registered trademark of Harlequin Mills & Boon Limited.